Jane and the Raven King

Jane and the Raven King

STEPHEN CHAMBERS

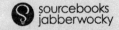
sourcebooks
jabberwocky

Published by Sourcebooks Jabberwocky, an imprint of Sourcebooks, Inc.
P.O. Box 4410, Naperville, Illinois 60567-4410
(630) 961-3900
Fax: (630) 961-2168
www.jabberwockykids.com

Library of Congress Cataloging-in-Publication data is on file with the publisher.

Source of Production: Webcom, Toronto, Ontario, Canada
Date of Production: October 2010
Run Number: 13730

Printed and bound in Canada.

WC 10 9 8 7 6 5 4 3 2 1

For Ellie

Contents

CHAPTER 1

Packing for a Trip

I don't believe it," Jane murmured.

Outside, a squirrel was wedged into a hole in the tree. *It's stuck,* Jane thought, but then the squirrel popped out with a little black box. Jane stopped copying her spelling words, checked to be sure Mrs. Alterman wasn't watching, and leaned on her desk for a better look. No, it wasn't a box; it was a suitcase. At first, Jane was sure she must be mistaken, but as she watched, the squirrel opened the tiny suitcase and began arranging nuts and acorns inside.

"Impossible."

Mrs. Alterman lowered her red pen and frowned. "Hm?"

"*Implacable,*" Jane said. "*I-M-P...*"

Mrs. Alterman said, "*Silently* please," and then returned to her grading. Jane glanced back out the window. The squirrel was packing in twitches and nervous half-starts, as if he were rushed and couldn't decide which nuts to leave and which to bring. He ducked back into the tree hole and returned with a scrap of blue fabric that he clutched to his furry chest for a long moment. Then he laid it carefully in the suitcase before closing the bag.

The bell rang.

"How far along are you, Jane?" Mrs. Alterman asked. "*Jane?*"

Jane said, "There's a squirrel…"

Mrs. Alterman took Jane's quiz to check the scribbled spelling words on the back as the kids came in loudly from recess. "You can finish the rest tomorrow. No more daydreaming like you did this morning. Get to class, Jane."

"But he has a suitcase—look."

"*A suitcase?*" Mrs. Alterman stepped closer to the window. The squirrel and his miniature black suitcase were gone. "Where?"

Michael approached behind Jane. "Is there something outside?"

Mrs. Alterman brightened. "Your sister has made friends with a squirrel," she said. "A squirrel with *luggage*."

Before Michael could speak, Jane said, "Mrs. Alterman, you saw him on the branch. He was right there."

"Why aren't you in class?" Michael said.

"Thank you, Michael," Mrs. Alterman said, and to Jane, "You can learn a lot from your younger brother. The first rule of success is punctuality. That's spelled *P-U*, Jane."

The class laughed, and Jane went into the hall just as the other teachers closed their doors. The bell rang again; she was late for math.

The day only got worse from there. After a lecture from Mr. Hendricks about how irresponsible and selfish it was to come to class late, she got a C- on her social studies test. Then she had to endure another language arts class, this time at the front of the class so Mrs. Alterman could smirk disapprovingly at Jane's doodled-on English book and call on her for every other question.

Between classes, Jane went to her locker alone. The inside door was stickered with a photo of a gorilla and environmental bumper stickers: *It's Not Easy Being Green* and *Save the Humans!*

Behind Jane, the leader of the popular girls, Alison, said, "What a loser. She doesn't even have a cell phone. Do you *know* what an iPod is, Jane?" Jane tried to ignore Alison and her friends, but Alison continued, "So, did you see the new episode last night? Oh, that's right—you don't watch TV." She nodded to a book. "Is that the stupid nature book you were reading by yourself at lunch? Is that worm on the cover one of your friends?"

Jane said, "*My* friends are worms? Look who's talking."

Alison slammed the locker, just missing Jane's fingers, and the girls all laughed as they left.

After school, Jane sat at the top of the steps outside the side entrance, and when the last of Michael's friends had been picked up, he joined her.

"So, you saw a talking squirrel?" he said.

"Shut up."

"Let's go get a soda," Michael said.

Two blocks off school property was a corner convenience store called Napps. It was a dingy shop across the street from the water treatment plant and Sadley Community College, and it sold everything from grinning green Buddha candles and switchblades to buckets of chlorine and soda. Jane checked her watch: 3:35. Their father wouldn't be there to pick them up until at least four o'clock.

"I don't want to," Jane said. "Dad told us not to leave the school grounds."

"It's only around the corner. Come on, I'm thirsty."

"No."

"Fine," he said and got up. "*I'm* going then."

"Michael…"

He started walking, so she reluctantly went with him. When they crossed through the school fence to a residential sidewalk, Michael said, "So, you had a bad day?"

"You could say that."

Jane watched the tree branches sway overhead, and her stomach clenched. The leaves rustled in the wind. She stopped.

Michael said, "What's up, Jane?"

"Something's wrong," she said. "Don't you feel that?"

"Feel what?"

"I don't know." Cars passed, and a pair of nannies walked by pushing baby strollers. They were both talking on cell phones.

"Come *on*," Michael said again. "I'm thirsty."

Jane nodded and continued with him to Napps, waiting by racks of candy bars and incense as Michael selected a drink from behind the sliding refrigerator door. *I did feel something*, Jane thought. *I noticed something, as if part of the world were off balance or had suddenly changed to a different color. But what?*

Michael bought his drink and said, "Are you going to tell me about the squirrel? What did Mrs. Alterman mean?"

Jane started to answer, then froze as they went back outside. A grizzled old man with white eyes—the frosted pupils of a blind man—was waiting with a fat German shepherd. The man wore a leather coat and blue cap, and he held the dog on a thick chain. Watching Michael's soda, the German shepherd whimpered, and Michael took Jane's arm as she stared at the old man's eyes.

"Do you know the name of the world?" the man said. "Did she tell you?"

Jane didn't move. "The name of the world—you mean *Earth?*"

"Do you know where it is?" He hobbled closer. "They will come for it very soon—do you understand?" The dog flopped onto his back, belly in the air, paws curled. "Well?" the old man said.

Jane said, "I'm sorry…?"

"He would like," the old man said gravely, "a tummy rub."

"Oh." Jane knelt to rub the German shepherd's belly, and the dog bicycled his hind legs, eyes closed as he wagged his tail and farted loudly.

Jane laughed. "He's cute."

"*Finn,*" the old man told the dog. "Mind your tail. She's only a child."

"Finn is a nice name," Jane said. "Is there something wrong with his tail?"

"He's a boxer," the old man said. "Very dangerous."

"A boxer? He looks like a German shepherd to me."

"A *tail* boxer," the old man said.

"*Jane,*" Michael said. "Come on."

"There isn't much time," the old man said, and he smiled, showing yellowish teeth. "But if you follow me, we may still stop him."

"Stop who?"

Michael pulled her arm again. "*Jane*."

The old man said, "The black heart of the world, the prince of justice made miserable, the broken one." When she didn't answer, he lowered his voice. "The Raven King."

"I'm sorry," Jane said. "I can't do that right now. I have to go."

"Please," the old man called after them. "You are in danger, both of you. *Finn*—mind your tail…"

When they'd walked a block, Michael said, "What is wrong with you? You're talking to crazy people in the street—what if he had tried to hurt you?"

"I'm sorry." Jane shook her head. "You're right." But the nervousness in her gut was back, and now her chest constricted, making it harder to breathe. Something *was* wrong.

"What would Mom and Dad say if they'd seen you talking to that crazy man and his dog?"

Jane forced a smile. "I didn't talk to the dog. You don't think it's possible a squirrel would—?" And she realized what it was.

"A squirrel would what?"

"I know what's wrong," she said. "The trees—everything is too quiet."

Michael didn't understand. "Too quiet?"

As they came back onto the school grounds, they saw their father, arms across his chest, leaning against his car. He was chatting with Mrs. Alterman.

"Oh, no," Michael said. "He came early."

Mrs. Alterman shouted, "There they are!"

Their father gestured to the backseat. "In the car—*now*."

Michael looked at Jane before they got in. "Too quiet...?"

"The animals," she said. "They're leaving."

CHAPTER 2

The Warning

When they pulled out of the parking lot, their father said, "How many times have I told you not to leave after school? Michael, you should know better—and Jane, I'm very disappointed. You're supposed to—" His phone rang, and he answered it. "Hello? Yes, okay. Uh-huh…"

Jane waited, and Michael sipped his soda until their father finished his conversation. *We're in for it,* Jane thought. Dad would probably yell for the entire twenty-minute car ride home, and they might even be grounded. But when their father ended his call, he drove in silence for a long moment, then turned up the music on the radio. Michael frowned at Jane, confused.

"Dad…?" Jane said.

"Yes, sweetie?"

"Are you…is everything okay?"

"Hm?" At a stop sign, he smiled into the backseat. "Sure. I'm sorry, were we talking about something before my phone rang? How was school?"

Suddenly pleased with himself, Michael said, "My day was good, but Jane—"

"I'm sorry, just a minute." Their father answered his cell phone again. "Oh, hi. Yes, I did see that email…"

As she listened to her father's call, the tension in Jane's belly worsened until she balled her fists and told herself to calm down. Everything was fine. Look, there was a bird in that tree right there and more in the sky, and there was a chipmunk in a flower patch. The animals weren't leaving; there was no squirrel with a suitcase; and so what if her dad was distracted? When he put his phone away again, their father began to hum along with the radio, tapping his fingers on the steering wheel. Michael grinned and enjoyed his soda. Jane rode in silence.

At home, Jane went to her room to feed celery to her pet iguana, Iz. After he'd eaten, she let him out of his tank to wander the bedroom. Jane's desk and chair were piled with papers, magazines, and softback books, the walls were covered with *National Geographic* posters, and a Chicago Cubs calendar hung beside her window. Lazy cars passed outside. Iz climbed onto Jane's lap. She stroked his head.

Michael knocked and came in. "What's the matter?"

"Dad didn't yell at us," Jane said.

"I know, isn't it great?"

"What's he doing now?"

"Working on his office computer." Michael smiled. "What will you do if your lizard poops on you?"

"Throw it at you."

"That's gross," he said. "Do you want to watch TV? Come on."

She started to protest, then put Iz back in his tank and joined Michael on the living room couch. Jane didn't usually watch television. *But maybe it will get my mind off everything,* she thought.

Television didn't help, and after the first program ended, she went back into her room to do her homework. *I'm being silly,* she told herself. *Silly and stupid, that's all.*

Jane stopped by Iz's tank. The iguana was sleeping against the glass, one eye half-open.

"Michael!" she called. "This isn't funny!"

There were words scrawled in the sand of the tank: HE IS COMING.

CHAPTER 3

Grandma Diana

"But I didn't write it!"

Jane slammed the door on Michael, let Iz roam again, and sat at her desk to work.

"You're so dumb!" Michael shouted from the other side of the door. "I didn't do it, Jane!"

"I don't care. Go away."

Jane hunched over her schoolbooks. Spelling words to memorize, twenty-two math problems on page 165—and she had to get that social studies test signed. What was that noise? She looked up. Iz was scratching the window. He'd never done that before. As she watched, the iguana slipped his claws under the window, jammed his snout into the gap, and began to wedge the window open.

"Oh, no, you don't," Jane said. She put Iz on the floor, then closed and locked the window. That was strange. Because it was still chilly outside, Jane's window was always shut. Someone had unlocked it.

Before she could start on her homework again, Iz climbed back to the window and resumed scratching, so Jane put him back in his tank and stirred up the sand to cover the words. *Who is coming?* she wondered. Who had Michael meant? It didn't make sense. That crazy blind man with his dog? The old man had talked about someone else—some kind of bird. The Raven King, wasn't it? That was nonsense, she should just worry about how to spell *capricious*. C-A-P...

Jane lost track of the time and was just finishing the last math problem when the doorbell chimed. She went to see who it was and came into the entryway just as her mother and father opened the front door. Michael stood back with Jane.

"Mom?" Jane said. "I didn't know you were home." Her mother always gave the kids a kiss when she got home and asked them what they wanted for dinner...

"Yes," her mother murmured. "Hi, honey."

Grandma Diana—her mother's mother—was waiting on the porch. Beautiful and strong like a warhorse or lioness, Grandma Diana wore a navy suit and carried a beaded purse. She was in town for a month, visiting all the way from England.

"There we are," she said with a slight British accent. "You both look pale. Are you feeling well?"

"Yes, Mother. It's good to see you," Jane's mother said. "Come in please."

Grandma Diana stepped in, handed her coat to Jane's father, and nodded approvingly at Jane. "This is how children are *meant* to look. Jane, you are lovelier than ever." Jane hugged her grandmother, and Grandma Diana raised her eyebrows at Michael. "What have we done now, Michael? Why the guilty look?"

"Nothing," he said. "I didn't do anything."

"I see." Her arm around Jane, Grandma Diana took them into

the living room and said, "I do not smell anything cooking. Am I early? You did say six-thirty, didn't you?"

"I am so sorry," Jane's mother said. "It completely slipped my mind…"

"Things have been so crazy," her father said.

"You forgot that I had been invited to dinner?" Grandma Diana asked, suddenly suspicious. She released Jane to examine Jane's parents. This wasn't like them, Jane thought. They'd never forgotten to prepare a meal before. Grandma Diana said, "You still intended to eat with your children, didn't you?"

"I am so sorry, Mother," Jane's mother said again.

"We forgot," her father said. "Honestly."

His phone rang. When he started to answer, Grandma Diana snatched it away and said, "Yes, who is this? He is busy feeding his family at the moment. You will have to try again tomorrow. Yes, I said tomorrow. Thank you, good night." She ended the call and drew herself up. "Now, then, I am partial to chicken fried rice. What would everyone else like?"

Jane's mother said, "Mother, we don't have the ingredients—"

"It is too late to cook," Grandma Diana announced. "Therefore, I am ordering Chinese food. Young Michael's favorite, if I am not mistaken. What would you like?"

Jane's father paled. "My phone…"

Michael wanted Mongolian beef, Jane asked for vegetable fried rice, her mother chose beef with broccoli, and her father continued to frown at his seized cell phone.

"My phone…" he said again.

"I doubt you could add enough soy sauce to make it edible," Grandma Diana said, and Michael laughed. "In any event," she continued, "I know for a fact that your fortune is not hidden inside. What would you like to eat?"

He said, "Shrimp teriyaki please."

"Right." Grandma Diana placed the order, returned his phone, and started for the kitchen. "Jane, please help me make tea, will you? Everyone else, have a seat. We will be back in a moment."

In the kitchen, Grandma Diana started rummaging through the cabinets, and when she heard the television come on in the living room, she called, "No TV! Turn it off, please! Thank you!" The television went silent. "Jane, dear, will you get the stove on and fill up the kettle?"

Jane clicked on the electric burner, rinsed out her mother's green teapot, and waited for the pot to fill in the sink.

"How is school, dear?" Grandma Diana asked.

"It's okay," Jane said.

Grandma Diana found three mugs, a can of tea leaves, and an ornate metal strainer. "I didn't have much use for it when I was your age either. Children see things much more clearly than adults. It's why adults are so difficult."

"Why?" Jane asked.

"They are jealous." Grandma Diana smiled. "That is enough water, dear. Put it on the stove please." Jane did, and as they waited for the water to boil, Grandma Diana arranged the three mugs on a tray decorated with pictures of cheese and French writing. She said, "Adults forget that they were small once. They forget the things they knew." She stared at the tray for a long moment, then forced another smile and put her arm around Jane. "You are good,

Jane, and very strong. Stronger than you know. Stronger than any of us, I think."

"School isn't *that* bad," Jane said.

"I am not talking about school. I am talking about *this*." Grandma Diana nodded to the empty kitchen and gave Jane a knowing look. "Something is wrong, isn't it? Don't pretend you don't understand. You know what I mean. Something is coming, and I feel as though…" She frowned as if she'd forgotten what she was going to say. "I should know what it is. It is familiar…"

The pot steamed and began to whistle. Grandma Diana lowered the heat, unscrewed the lid of the can, and sprinkled tea-leaf debris into the strainer, which she wedged over the first mug.

"When I was your age, the world seemed cruel and magnificent at the same time," she said as she carefully poured the boiling water through the strainer, filling the first mug. "Does it feel that way again?"

Jane watched her grandmother move the strainer to the second mug. "I don't know."

"There is no right or wrong answer, Jane. How does the world feel? Wonderful at times?"

"Yes."

"But at any moment…" She started pouring the third mug. "Ah, I am sure it is nothing. I am being foolish. Don't listen to me." She finished pouring and smiled. "Will you get the honey and milk, dear?"

Jane carried the tea tray into the living room, and Grandma Diana said, "Only the women will be drinking tea today."

Jane's mother and father had been staring at their reflections in the television while Michael flipped through a comic book.

"But I want tea too," he said.

"Are you a woman?" Grandma Diana said.

"No, but—"

"I am sure you would prefer a soft drink. Go ahead."

As her brother went into the kitchen, Jane arranged the tray on the center table, and Grandma Diana handed a mug to Jane's mother.

"I'm sorry," Jane's mother said. "Did you say something?"

"The tea is hot, dear," Grandma Diana said. "Don't burn yourself."

What is wrong with my parents? Jane wondered. *It's as if they can't even think straight.*

"Hold your tea out like this," Grandma Diana told Jane, raising her cup with both hands like an offering. "You too," she said to Jane's mother. When all three mugs were up, Grandma Diana said, "Come what may, let the warmth of this cup protect our dear Jane. Come what may." She paused. "That's all. Who would like honey?"

"Why is Jane so special?" Michael asked from the kitchen doorway.

"She is your sister," Grandma Diana said. "Isn't that enough of a reason?"

"Were you praying?"

Grandma Diana patted the couch beside her, and Michael came to sit there. "We are a family, Michael. Do you understand what that means?"

He slurped his soda. "Yes. But why were you praying for Jane?"

"Do you ever ask for things inside your head? For a good grade on a test or for a girl to like you?" He looked skeptical, but she continued, "That is all I was doing. I want good things for all of you because I love you very much. Now, where is our food?"

CHAPTER 5

The Storm

Thunder crashed, and they all jumped. Outside, it was suddenly much darker. Now, as Jane watched out the living room window, a wall of fast-moving blackness approached from across the street until hard rain lashed the windows. The wind chimes on the back porch rattled and clanged, and lightning flickered through the storm clouds. Jane's father had called thunder the sound of angels bowling, and as it smashed again, she wondered if one of them had hit a strike.

"Cool," Michael said.

"Now where did all that come from?" Jane's mother said.

"The TV," Grandma Diana said. "Let's turn it on."

Michael looked pleased. "I thought you said we weren't supposed to watch—"

"Quiet, Michael," Grandma Diana snapped. Jane's mother turned on the television. A red crawl at the top of the screen told them that there was a severe thunderstorm warning and a tornado watch.

"Change it to cartoons," Michael said.

Jane's father murmured, "We should get to the basement."

Grandma Diana sighed, and Michael gave Jane a funny look. Their mother patted their father's hand. "We don't have a basement, dear," she said. "Remember?"

Hypnotized by the television, he nodded. "Oh. I knew that, didn't I?"

"Right," Grandma Diana said. "Switch it off please."

Jane's mother held the remote control, but she didn't budge. "Just one minute."

They were watching a fast-food commercial. Wind and rain thrashed the windows, and thunder grumbled again.

"Give me the remote," Grandma Diana said.

Jane's mother moved away, as if she were going to sit on it. "Not yet..."

"Mom," Jane said. "What's the matter? It's just a commercial."

"I'm sorry," her mother said, frowning as if she were struggling to look away from the screen. "I can't turn it off right now."

"That's right," Jane's father said. "Leave it on."

"Let's watch cartoons," Michael said again. "Mom, can you change the channel at least?"

Grandma Diana stood and extended her hand, as if Jane's mother were a dog that had stolen her shoe. "Give it to me."

"I can't," Jane's mother said.

Jane said, "Mom..." But when she reached out, her mother jerked away to protect the remote.

"*Now*," Grandma Diana said.

"Mom..."

"Do not touch her, Jane."

"No," Jane's mother said, but she still hadn't looked up from the TV screen.

Michael said, "I don't understand—"

Grandma Diana clapped her hands and shouted, "*Aven saat!*" At that, lightning struck a power line across the street in a burst of glittery sparks and a *crack* like an aluminum bat smacking a metal trash can. The lights went out, and the TV blipped to black.

Michael jumped up and said, "Grandma, how did you *do* that?"

Grandma Diana ignored him, watching Jane's mother, who blinked and finally looked up. "I'm sorry," Jane's mother said. "Did you say something?"

"It's fine, dear," Grandma Diana said and took the remote. She crouched behind the entertainment center and unplugged the power cords.

"We lost power," Jane's father said. "I'd better check the circuit breakers and get flashlights." He paused as if he'd forgotten something, then asked Grandma Diana, "Is everything all right?"

"Yes, everything's fine." Grandma Diana sat with Jane's mother. "Jane, take your brother and find batteries."

Jane and Michael went into the kitchen, and Michael said, "Did you *see* that?"

"Lightning struck the power line."

"She *made* it hit the power line," he said.

"Maybe," Jane said.

"What do you mean *maybe?* That was so cool. I want to know how she did it."

Jane found three boxes of unopened batteries in the drawer with the rubber bands and scissors.

"Something's wrong with Mom and Dad," she said.

"What?"

"I don't know, but you saw how they were acting."

Michael started to answer, but then his faced flushed. "I can't play on my computer now that the power's out, can I?"

"Michael, I think this is important."

"I was supposed to get this new game tonight." He kicked the drawer shut. "This is so annoying."

She led him back into the living room. "Come on."

"There we are," Grandma Diana said. "Batteries, as requested."

"All right, hand them here," Jane's father said, organizing flashlights and lamps on the carpet. "Let's find out how many of these work."

"Should we call the restaurant?" Jane's mother asked. "They may not deliver in this weather."

Rain raked the windows, and her father grinned. "Tonight, they'll earn their tip."

They're back, Jane thought. *My parents are back to normal. It was nothing; they were just distracted.* Grandma Diana met her stare with a knowing expression.

The doorbell chimed.

"*Finally!*" Michael said.

The food had arrived.

CHAPTER 6

The Gift

After a terrific dinner, Michael asked what they were going to do with the power still out. Grandma Diana pulled a deck of cards from her purse.

"Pinochle," she said.

"Don't you think they're a little young?" Jane's mother asked.

"Nonsense," Grandma Diana said. "I am certain Michael's favorite game is far more complicated." She nodded to him. "Isn't that true—what is your favorite game?"

"On the computer?" he asked.

"On anything."

"Well, there's this one game I was supposed to play tonight, but now I'm not going to be able to…"

Their father frowned. "And where were you going to get it?"

"On my *computer*," Michael said.

"But who was going to buy it for you?"

"You don't have to *buy it*," Michael said. "He was going to give it to me for free."

Grandma Diana set down the cards. "Who?"

Michael hesitated, suddenly uncomfortable with everyone watching him. "No one."

"I told you about talking to people on the Internet," their father said. "How many times have I said that?"

"Not on *the Internet*," Michael said.

"Michael," Grandma Diana said calmly. "No one is angry with you. We are only curious about your new game."

"I can't even describe it," Michael said, his face lighting up again. Rain pounded and thrashed outside. "It looked so cool, like so much fun."

"A man was going to give this game to you?" their mother asked.

"Not a man," Michael said. "A boy—one of our neighbors."

Their parents relaxed, but Grandma Diana asked, "What is the boy's name?"

"Nolan."

Her face hardened, and Jane noticed one of Grandma Diana's fists squeezing the card box.

"So pinochle it is," their father said. "I'm a little rusty. Let's go over the rules."

Grandma Diana nodded, the cold tension gone again, and she said, "Everyone pay attention. Pinochle is a game with a long tradition of sore losers. We do not want any in this house, so we will be perfectly clear on the rules before we begin. Now then…"

They played five games. Their mother won the first two, then Michael won, then Jane, and, finally, their father came out ahead in the last game.

"I thought I had lost my touch," he said, as Grandma Diana put the cards away. "But I guess I just needed to warm up."

Grandma Diana stood. "Well played. And it is late. I had better be getting back to my hotel."

"In this?" Jane's mother said. "It's terrible outside. You're not driving in this weather."

They all went to the window to watch the thunderstorm. Lightning streaked in the blackness overhead, followed by a low wave of thunder.

"I am sure it will be fine," Grandma Diana said. "I have driven in worse."

"I won't have you out in this storm, Mother."

Before Grandma Diana could object again, the town's air-raid sirens came on—meaning tornadoes had been spotted—and she smiled, surrendering to her daughter's better judgment. They all got ready for bed. Jane fed Iz and was about to brush her teeth when Grandma Diana knocked and came into her bedroom.

"I like your friend here," Grandma Diana said. "I've always had a soft spot for rabbits, but I like lizards too. His name's Iz, isn't it? A good name—it suits him."

"Thank you," Jane said. Kids at school and Michael always mocked her iguana's name. She'd gotten it from the name of a Hawaiian musician her father liked.

"Before I forget," Grandma Diana said, "I have something for you." She took a small jewelry box from her purse. "A present."

"Thank you," Jane said again.

"It isn't much. Open it."

Jane popped off the lid. Wedged into a bed of white foam was a purple stone with blue sparkles at its center. Although it was smooth like a large marble, it wasn't perfectly round.

"It is a good luck stone," Grandma Diana said. "Keep it with you."

Jane took it out and rolled it in her palm. It was heavier than it looked. She didn't know how to respond. It was just a *rock*, after all—but there was something about the glitter at its core...

"Thank you," Jane said.

"You are disappointed?"

"No," Jane said. "It's pretty, I like it—thank you, Grandma."

"It was given to me when I was your age. Your mother never had any use for it, but you... Keep it with you, and only break it if you absolutely must." She kissed Jane's forehead. "Good night, dear. Get some sleep."

"Good night, Grandma."

Grandma Diana turned to go, and there was Michael, watching from the hall.

"You are as quiet as a mouse, Michael," Grandma Diana said as she walked out. "Sleep well."

"Good night," he said. Then, he came into Jane's room. "What'd she give you?" Jane showed him the stone, and he said, "What is it?"

"Just a rock," she said. "I think."

"I hope the power comes on. Are you sleepy?"

"Yes, it's late."

"Well, I'm not," he said and went back into the hall. "But this stupid storm..."

Jane put on her pajamas and arranged the stone on her dresser. She brushed her teeth, said good night to her parents, and then got into bed. For some reason, she found herself staring at Grandma Diana's stone. *Just a rock,* she told herself. But then, without thinking, she grabbed the stone and slipped it under her pillow. She was afraid and didn't know why. She listened to the rain and closed her eyes. That was funny, wasn't it? *Sleeping with a rock under my pillow,* Jane thought. *Funny.*

CHAPTER 7

In the Night

12:00.

Jane's alarm clock was blinking red.

12:00.

She rolled over, pulled the covers up, shivering in a wet chill.

Wet...? She sat up.

12:00. 12:00.

The window was open. Rain spattered the wall, and her schoolbooks, the magazines on her desk—they were all getting soaked. She got up, shut the window, and turned the lock. I closed the window, Jane thought. This afternoon, I locked it.

Maybe it was broken. She watched the dark bedroom and listened to the wind suck and shake outside. Her door was open. Jane always shut her bedroom door at night in case Iz snuck out of his tank. Iz...the iguana was standing on his hind legs facing the open bedroom door and dark hallway. Jane's pulse quickened. She told herself to calm down. *The window lock is broken,* she thought. *And the wind blew open the door.* Except that the window would need to be *pushed*—it couldn't fall up and open on its own. Had someone opened it? *Michael,* she thought, *it must be Michael. This is some kind of joke—he's trying to scare me.*

Jane went to her bedroom door, started to close it, and stopped. Michael's door was closed, but she could see a faint light under the bottom. Now that the power was back on, he had woken up to play computer games or something. *So why did he open my window?* she wondered. *It doesn't matter. Shut the door, and go back to sleep.*

Iz scratched the lid of his tank, and Jane pressed her door closed. It creaked. She caught it and held it open. Had she just heard a woman's voice?

Jane held her breath and listened to her heartbeat, loud in both ears. Iz was scratching harder now. *No, I'm tired,* she thought. *I didn't*—But there it was again: the murmur of a woman's voice. Jane stepped into the hall and crept toward the kitchen doorway that would give her a view into the living room. *This is stupid,* she told herself. *Someone is probably watching TV, that's all.* Breathing faster, Jane reached the doorway. Past the kitchen, she could see Grandma Diana seated upright on the living room couch, hands folded in her lap. She was whispering, and as Jane watched, she noticed a white-blue glare around her grandmother. It was as if Grandma Diana were backlit by a soft lamp so she appeared to glow.

"Grandma?" Jane said.

Grandma Diana stopped speaking and cocked her head toward the kitchen. Something moved in the darkness near the TV.

"Grandma?" Jane said again.

"Go back to your room, Jane," Grandma Diana said. "Shut the door."

"Are you all right?"

"I am fine. Please go back to your room, dear."

Jane hesitated. "Grandma…"

A stalk-thin shadow moved into the kitchen with halting steps, as if on stilts. The stickman was black and huge, and as it approached her, Jane stumbled backward into the wall.

"Grandma!"

"You will not touch her!" Grandma Diana shouted, and a bulb of white-blue light flashed between Jane and the stickman. In the sudden light, the kitchen and living room were illuminated, and Jane saw many more—dozens—of shadow stickmen. They were hugging the walls like human insects, their long limbs ponderous, their faceless heads dented with hollow eyes. The stickmen moaned like the ocean.

Grandma Diana began to whisper again—it wasn't English, but it drew the shadows toward her, away from Jane. Jane was trembling. Her legs wouldn't work, and she gasped, fighting to breathe.

"Your room, Jane," Grandma Diana said.

Michael's door opened, and as yellow light spilled into the hall, Jane heard the *click-clack-click* of his computer keys. A boy stepped out. Behind the boy, Michael sat with his back to Jane, frantically playing a computer game.

"Can I get you anything?" the boy asked Jane as he shut Michael's door.

She smelled finger paint and glue, and she shuddered as if she'd been pushed and was too ashamed of her own helplessness to respond. That smell: *A memory from my childhood,* Jane thought. *Children laughed at me, a teacher ridiculed me, and when I broke down, I buried my face in those smells.* The odor brought it all back now. And just as quickly, it was gone.

"No?" the boy said. "Excuse me then."

He stepped past Jane into the kitchen, and she lost sight of him. Then she heard the rustling of heavy wings and glimpsed a shadow on the ceiling above Grandma Diana.

"Child," the bird-shadow said. "I will ask you once: where is it?"

Grandma Diana looked up, the light around her stronger now. "None of them know. I have told no one."

A low laugh came, and although Jane couldn't see the stickmen, she heard them moan again.

"*Where?*"

Grandma Diana stood, raised one arm, and said, "When I break you, your evil will die and never return. You will be forgotten."

"Forgotten?" the bird-shadow said, and Jane heard wings flap like the branches of a great tree. "You are afraid."

Grandma Diana's light dilated, then crackled into glowing barbs that caught the stickmen as if they were metal rods. She raised her fist, shouting in another language—"*Ignatio vate!*"—as fire burst from her knuckles and flowed into the great black bird over her. The bird screamed and flailed, the stickmen shrank, and Grandma Diana yelled, "Run, Jane!" before the bird shook away the flames and descended on her. Grandma Diana crumpled to the floor. Her light went out.

Jane ran into the living room. "Grandma!" Grandma Diana

wasn't breathing. Her skin was shrinking like wet paper. There were big blue marbles where her eyes should have been, and her hair wasn't real—it was fake hair. The skin wasn't skin anymore—it was plastic. Jane was holding a giant toy: a mannequin of her grandmother. A hand stroked Jane's chin, and she looked up. The boy from Michael's room smiled at her.

"Where is it?" he said. "She must have told you. I only want to see it."

"I don't know what you're talking about," Jane said.

The boy was losing his patience, and Jane glimpsed a rotten, hooked beak and empty, animal eyes. Then he was just a boy with none of those other things. "The name of the world," he said. "What did she do with it?"

"What did you do to my grandmother?" Jane said. "Where is she?"

"You don't have a grandmother," he said. "You never did. She is that dead. Now, where is it?"

Jane smelled mold, but she stepped closer, right in his face. *He's just a boy,* she told herself. Anything else was impossible. "Where is my grandmother?"

"You will answer me—"

Jane slapped him. The room streaked and polarized—black to white, white to black—and when Jane blinked, the boy had staggered backward, blood on his lip. For a long second, he stared at her, shocked and terrified. Then, the air sucked, and he wasn't a boy anymore—he was a man in a bloody cape with huge wings and then a black bird as giant as the wall. Jane stumbled and ran.

The bird screamed, "Kill her!"

She threw open Michael's bedroom door. "Michael, come on!"

He didn't look away from his computer. "Hold on…"

She yanked him away from the screen. "We have to go."

"What is your problem—?" He saw the stickmen lumbering closer in the kitchen and ran with Jane into her bedroom.

The top of the iguana tank had fallen. Iz was gone.

"What *are* those things?" Michael said.

Jane shoved open her bedroom window, then glanced back as stickmen came into the hall. "I don't know." It was still raining outside. "But we have to go."

"What about Mom and Dad?"

"They'll be fine," Jane said, and she slipped one leg outside.

Michael was pale, but he didn't let go of her hand. "Where are we going?"

"I don't—"

A voice outside said, "This way."

The blind man and his dog waited in matching yellow raincoats. The man caught Jane's wrist and helped her down. "Quickly!" he said. "Quickly now! Finn, watch the front lawn."

Michael hesitated at the open window as a stickman ambled into the bedroom behind him.

"Hurry!" the blind man said. "Out, out!"

Michael said, "Jane…"

"It's all right," Jane said. "Give me your hand."

The stickman neared Michael, ten feet away. Now eight feet. Six.

"Michael, come on!" she shouted.

"That man with you is crazy," Michael said.

Four feet from Michael, the stickman stretched one formless hand toward his shoulder.

"*Now* Michael!"

"I—" He saw the stickman out of the corner of his eye and jerked backward, banging his head on the window as he somersaulted out. Jane and the blind man caught him. Shaking in the wet grass, Michael said, "Now what are we supposed to—?"

The stickman slipped one arm out the window. Its shadow-head and torso followed, then a leg, and the blind man said, "Run!"

CHAPTER 8

New Acquaintances

After sprinting three blocks, they stopped, panting and drenched, outside a parked RV camper. Painted in khaki-brown desert camouflage, the mobile home looked as though it had dropped from the sky or been hauled out with the driveway garbage cans.

The blind man opened the RV door and said, "Watch your step."

"Are you nuts?" Michael said. "We're not going with you."

"It's pouring rain," Jane said, but she didn't follow the blind man. *Sure, our clothes are already soaked through,* she thought, wiping strands of hair from her eyes, *but who is this blind man?*

"We don't know him!" Michael shouted to her over the thunder.

The rain hammered them, and Jane hugged her dripping shirt. "What's your name?" she asked the blind man.

He cupped a hand to his ear. "Eh?" The dog, Finn, hopped into the camper to wait, his tail wagging.

"Your name?"

"My name is Gaius," he said.

"*Gaius?*" Michael said. "What kind of name is that? Jane, what are we doing out here? We should go back."

"Let me think," Jane said, pacing in the rain. "I'm sorry, Mr. Gaius, but my brother is right. We don't know you…"

"You can't go home," Gaius said, as if that were obvious. "It's too dangerous now. We have to leave before they follow you."

"And go where?" Michael said.

"Where do you think?" Gaius said. "To Hotland."

Jane shook her head. "'Hotland?' Where—?"

"Where else? At the center of the Earth. Now watch your step. The stairs are wet."

"He's crazy," Michael said. "We're not going with him."

Jane turned to her brother. "You let that boy, *Nolan*, in through my window, didn't you?"

"What?"

"You did, didn't you?"

"No, why would I do that?"

But the way he looked away and crossed his arms meant he was lying. "Grandma Diana is dead because of you!" Jane said. "And why—for a computer game?"

"Grandma Diana isn't dead," Michael said, and he sneezed in the rain. "Come on, let's go home."

"I can't believe you did that."

"Did what?"

"Wake up, Michael! We are standing in a thunderstorm because your friend let a bunch of shadow people into our home—"

"*Sansi*," Gaius said. "They're properly called sansi—stickmen."

Jane jerked her fist down. She wanted to slap Michael the way she'd rattled that monster-boy, Nolan. "You're not stupid," Jane said. "You *knew*, but you wanted a new game."

"Shut up," Michael said. "I don't believe you. Grandma Diana isn't dead, and there's no such thing as stickmen."

Jane said, "You *saw* them!"

"No, I didn't."

Gaius said, "*Nolan* is an old joke. It's a trickster name."

Michael said, "I don't care."

"What does it mean?" Jane asked.

Gaius said, "What does it sound like?"

Jane said it: "Nolan, Nolan, No-lan." She shivered in the rain. "It sounds like *no one.*"

"Exactly."

"That's dumb," Michael said. "It's just a name."

"But it isn't *his* name," Gaius said. "He hasn't had a real name in a long time. The Raven King is a broken god, not a boy or even a bird. He is something else entirely. He is the old wickedness at the heart of the world."

"I don't care," Michael said again. "I'm going home."

"You cannot," Gaius said.

Jane said, "Michael…"

"No, I don't believe any of this. I was dreaming or something."

Jane grabbed his shoulder, but Michael shook her away. "Please," she said.

"Go with your new friend," Michael said.

"Don't be stupid. Those things are probably still there."

"What things?"

"The stickmen."

Michael walked away. "I don't know what you're talking about."

"Let him go," Gaius said. "Jane, please let him go. I need your help." He paused. "I know why the animals are leaving."

Jane hesitated, but Michael was walking faster. She smiled at Gaius and his dog. "Thank you, but I'm sorry. I have to go with him—I can't let him go back alone." As she hurried after Michael, Jane heard Gaius mutter to his dog. As she caught up to Michael, she said to him, "You are *so* stubborn sometimes."

Their house came into view at the end of the next block. All the lights were on.

CHAPTER 9

Severe Weather

Jane stopped on the front lawn and grabbed her brother's shoulder. "Wait."

"Make me."

It's late and still raining, Jane thought. *Mom and Dad must be worried. That's why all the lights are on. But what if something else is going on? Should we walk in the front door?*

"Michael, stop."

He stepped onto the porch and said, "You stop."

"Don't—"

He rang the doorbell.

Jane went to stand beside him on the floral doormat. At least the front porch was out of the rain. When no one answered, Michael pressed the button again, and they heard the doorbell chime in the entry hall. Still no answer. *Something is wrong,* Jane thought. Even in the upstairs bathroom with the shower running, they should be able to hear the doorbell.

"Let's go," she said.

Michael frowned and jabbed the button again.

"Michael, let's go."

"The lights are on," he said.

"That doesn't mean—" Jane shivered as she noticed the

surrounding houses. They looked like ships made out of brick and glass in the midnight rain. All the windows glowed through blinds and drapes—the porches bathed in fuzzy white light. *All the lights are on,* Jane thought. *In every house on the block. In the middle of the night.*

"Come on," she said.

"No. You can go stand in the rain if you want."

"Don't ring the doorbell again."

After he did anyway, Michael shrugged. "Maybe it's broken."

"It's not broken—we can hear it."

"Let go of my arm," he said. "I'll climb back in the window."

"Michael, listen to me—"

"Shut up."

When he tried to push past her, Jane blocked him, and Michael grabbed the doorknob. It turned, and the door opened. As it creaked wide, Michael hesitated. The hall light, the lamps—even the upright flashlights on the plant table were lit. Men talked seriously in the living room—it was the television—and Jane heard at least one radio voice deeper inside the house, along with the background rhythm of reggae music.

"This isn't right," she said.

"Don't be stupid." Michael stepped inside. "Are you coming?"

No, Jane thought. Every part of her—especially the jittery hollow in her belly—told her to walk away. *Don't go in.* But Michael was already in the main hall, calling, "Mom? Dad—we're back!"

Jane came in and shut the front door behind her. "Michael…"

He disappeared around the corner, heading for the kitchen. Jane's pulse quickened as she crept into the entry hall. As she edged closer to the main hall, she checked the living room; the lamps were on, and the ceiling fan whipped like a helicopter blade, shaking the yellow overhead lights. Grandma Diana was gone. Cowboys from a grainy Western murmured solemnly on the television, and the shot panned across a desert vista of cacti and sunset rock mesas. She heard one of the cowboys say, "Round 'em up."

"All of them? Ain't time for that."

"Keep the women inside and round 'em up…"

From the kitchen, Michael shouted, "Mom! Where are you?"

Jane went into the main hall, and Michael returned, his face pale. "Did you see Mom and Dad?" he asked.

"No," Jane said. "We have to get out of here."

Michael stepped past her, heading for the stairs. "Mom? Dad?"

"Michael, stop it."

He started upstairs, and she ran after him. "Michael—"

They froze near the top. From the end of the second-floor hall, they heard the click of a keyboard and the staccato drone of a radio reporter's voice. All the lights were on here too: the hall lights, the lights in her father's office—in the bathroom, even the electric-socket night-lights were lit. Michael opened his mouth and shut it again.

Jane whispered, "Come on."

He ignored her and walked down the hall. "Mom…?"

No answer.

Jane's heartbeat throbbed in her ears. "Stop it," she said. "Please…"

"Mom?" Michael said again, and he crept toward their parents' open bedroom door.

I can't leave him, Jane told herself and watched Michael near the bedroom doorway. The keyboard-radio noises were coming from in there.

"Mom?" Michael said.

When Jane mouthed, "No!" he continued inside, looked at the bed, and stiffened.

Jane went after him. Their parents sat on the king-size bed, laptop computers on their legs, cell phones wedged between their ears and shoulders. Their father even had a cordless phone pushed against his right ear. The voice on the alarm clock radio said, *"...A flash flood warning is in effect for Mercer County until 3:00 a.m. Winds are expected to exceed forty miles an hour, with severe gusts in excess of sixty miles an hour possible. A tornado watch is in effect until..."*

Michael said, "Mom? Dad?"

Both of their parents pounded their laptop keys. Their father cleared his throat into the phone and grunted, "Uh-huh. Um."

"Dad?" Michael said again.

"...Residents are advised to avoid unnecessary travel and to stay tuned for further advisories. In the event a tornado is spotted, proceed immediately to the basement or to an interior, windowless room..."

Thunder cracked, and rain battered the bedroom window. Jane held her brother's hand.

"Dad," she said. "Are you okay?"

He didn't look up.

Michael began to tremble. "Jane…"

Jane stepped closer to the bed. "Mom?"

"Uh-huh," she said into her phone. "Okay."

When they still didn't stop typing, Jane clapped her hands in front of her father's computer screen—he was closer—and he frowned, as if she were a stranger. Slowly, he noticed them.

"Jane, Michael," he said and returned to his keyboard.

"Mom, Dad, stop it," Jane said.

They didn't look up.

She slammed her father's laptop shut and braced for his irritated shout. But he didn't shout. Instead, he blinked at her, *through* her, his mind elsewhere.

"…This is a severe weather alert for Harrison County," the radio said. "A flash flood warning is in effect…"

"We have to go," Jane said.

"I'm not leaving." Before Jane could argue, Michael said, "If you want to, then go. I'm going to bed, and when I wake up, all this will be back to normal."

"Michael—"

"Get away from me." He ran downstairs to his room and slammed the door. Jane knew that when he was like this, it was pointless to argue—Michael was too stubborn. *I can't just leave him here,* she thought and went downstairs.

"Please Michael," she called. "Don't—"

"Go away!"

I have no idea where to go, Jane thought. But that wasn't true, and she knew it.

CHAPTER 10

Places to Go

Still wearing a yellow poncho, Gaius met her in the street. "We don't have much time," he said. "Does your grandmother still live in England?"

"She's dead," Jane said. "I *saw* it." Jane's voice twisted when she said this, and she felt tears behind her eyes. Talking about the horrible, impossible murder suddenly made it real. She lost her balance on a sewer grate, and Gaius caught her.

"Be careful around pipes," he said. "All pipes lead to Hotland."

"I don't understand."

"It's all right," he said, but she could tell from the drop in his voice that it wasn't.

They went to Gaius's RV. He opened the door and ushered her inside Like a bric-a-brac shop on wheels, the camper was crammed with junk: bicycle wheels; stone statues with lamps attached to their heads; afghan blankets of red, orange, and yellow-green; a pile of water-stained road maps; a tiny television with contorted antennae; jars of motionless butterflies; and mounds of ivory dice—some with the usual six sides Jane recognized from Monopoly and dozens more with intricate, tiny numbers and symbols. One die was as large as a tennis ball, divided into at least one hundred numbered sides. Painted model airplanes dangled from the ceiling, and the German shepherd, Finn, sprawled comfortably on a black couch matted with dog fur. There were snake skins, soccer balls, and a trash can overflowing with crumpled, used tissue.

"Have a seat," Gaius said. "Finn, get up. Make some room—you don't need the whole couch to yourself. Up, up already!"

Finn rose slowly, stretching his limbs until every joint—including those in his fluffy toes—popped. Then he sat, licked his lips, yawned, and farted. Finn hopped off the couch, and as he looked for a suitable place on the floor, Jane could've sworn she saw the dog smirk back over his shoulder. *No,* she told herself. *Dogs do not smirk.* Even stubborn, flatulent dogs forced to surrender comfy couches didn't smirk.

"He takes up a lot of space," Jane said.

"Yes, well." Gaius glared as Finn thumped dramatically onto a pile of old coats in the corner. "Be grateful he's only a dog."

"What does that mean?" Jane asked.

"Sit," Gaius said, and he went into the front cabin. "Your brother…?"

"He wouldn't come," Jane said. "Will he be okay?"

Gaius ignored the question. "Hold on to something," he said. "I drive fast."

Wait a second, Jane thought. *Isn't he blind?*

There were no windows, but she could tell by the way the clutter-towers swayed that they were moving quickly. *What was I thinking?* she wondered. *This is crazy! I'm going to get myself killed! We might crash at any—*

The RV stopped.

Jane followed Gaius and Finn outside; they were parked near a dark stand of trees. The rain had stopped, and the air was thick, heavy, and silent.

Jane said, "How did you drive without…?"

"You don't need your eyes to drive," Gaius said. "You only need your hands for the steering wheel and your feet for the pedals."

"But—"

"We'll discuss this again when you have a driver's license, Jane." Finn lifted his leg on the nearest roots, and Gaius said, "Here, now—what kind of introduction is that, Finn? They'll whisper about that for half a mile."

"Where are we?" Jane asked.

"The park," Gaius said. He pressed his hand to a tree trunk, closed his eyes, and then glared at Finn. "You couldn't have used a bush?" They continued walking, and when Gaius stopped at another tree, he said, "We have to go underground to Hotland."

"By slapping trees? You're talking to them," Jane said, "aren't you?"

Gaius removed his hand. "Yes. Anyway, these trees have deep roots."

Jane stepped beside Gaius and placed her fingers on the rough bark. She closed her eyes and listened.

"I don't hear anything," she said.

Gaius resumed walking. "The trees don't trust you."

"Why not?"

Gaius frowned. "How many pieces of paper have you used? How many wooden chairs, tables, and bedposts have you used?"

"They think I'm going to chop them down?" Jane said.

Gaius said, "No, but they would like an occasional thank you. Written on recycled paper, I suppose."

Finn barked, his tail wagging.

"Ah." Gaius brightened. "He found one."

They hurried after Finn to a great, old oak tree. Gaius checked the trunk and nodded. Jane pressed her palm to the bark, but again, she didn't hear anything.

"Good." Gaius pointed his cane at the tree. "We are off then."

The center of the trunk darkened, as if it had been covered by a black towel. The darkness looked just as solid as the bark.

Gaius said, "I should warn you—we will have to cross the Keeper, but she hasn't stopped anyone in a thousand years. The Keeper is neutral. She watches what goes in and what comes out in order to protect Hotland. Everyone who enters has to cross her once. After that, you'll never see her again."

"What is she?" Jane asked.

Gaius stepped closer to the darkness. "Wait and see."

CHAPTER 11

The Keeper

Holding the flap of Gaius's coat, Jane followed him into the tree. Breathing hard, she could hear their footsteps—was the floor made of stone?—but she was as blind as the old man. The moment they stepped into the tree, it was as though they had fallen into a cave or a tomb. Even the entry-hole behind them was gone.

Jane heard Finn's paw nails clicking to her right, and she concentrated on the reassuring jingle of his collar. The darkness thinned ahead. They entered a room of stone statues, with a block pyramid in the center. The room was big—at least twice as tall as her entire house—and the walls were the same white marble as the floor. Where was the door? There was no way out, and now when Jane turned, she saw a blank wall behind them.

Still squeezing Gaius's coat, Jane followed him through the maze of statues. They passed a bearded man wearing some kind of loose dress and sandals, a stunted spear in his hands, then walked around a group of cowering Asiatic women with babies clutched in their robes and an ugly man in heavy armor with the legs of a goat. There were small men on horseback, bare-chested women chained in a line, and ape-men with high foreheads and stumpy noses.

"Who are they?" Jane asked.

Finn sprawled and licked himself.

Gaius said, "They are the people she stopped."

"They're real people?"

"They were—a long time ago, when they tried to enter Hotland. They are stone now."

"I don't like this," Jane said.

"Not so loud," Gaius said.

"Why, what…?"

Finn jumped up. Something moved at the top of the pyramid: a thick silver shape like a beast climbing out of the pyramid's bricks.

Jane was trembling. She watched the muscular flank rise, saw a tuft of brilliant hair, and the creature shook itself and looked down at them. It was a horse—a horse the size of a school bus. Its skin shimmered like the moon; its mane was solid gold, and it stared with cruel eyes that glowed the hot white of a furnace fire. On its forehead was the broken stump of a horn. When the Keeper—the unicorn—shifted its weight, sparks snapped under its hooves. It spoke with a strained woman's voice, as if it had been screaming: "What is your name?"

"What do you—?"

"Speak quickly," the unicorn told Jane. "What is your name?"

"Jane."

"Your grandmother, Diana Starlight, is gone?"

Diana Starlight? Jane thought, but she said, "Yes."

The unicorn snorted and tossed her head, as if she were shaking away a fly. "How old are you?"

"Almost thirteen."

"Do you believe there are such things as good and evil?"

Jane swallowed, her palms clammy, her pulse jittery and fast. *Answer—no, think: What do I believe? Do I really believe in good and evil?* Although Jane had been baptized and her parents took the kids to church occasionally—usually on Christmas and Easter—she never thought of herself and certainly never considered her parents religious. There was right and wrong, wasn't there? Was that the same thing?

"Answer me, Jane," the unicorn rumbled. "Do good and evil exist?"

"I don't know," she said.

"What principle binds the world?"

Gaius lowered his head and said, "Honored Keeper, she is only—"

"I am not addressing you, Gaius Saebius."

"Please," he said, "she is no threat to you—she is only a child."

"She is no child." The unicorn's eyes flashed. "Speak again unprompted, and it will be for the last time. There is more in her than there was in Diana Starlight or Applepatch Mary. I must know, Jane, what is the binding principle of existence?"

"I don't know that."

"Do not lie to me. How do you see the world—is it ruled by order or chaos?"

Trembling, Jane thought, *Michael was right—I shouldn't have come here. This isn't real.*

She said, "I'm sorry, I don't—"

"If you do not answer, you will join my gallery."

Jane said, "Please…" And she turned to run.

"Stop!"

She froze, struggled to catch her breath. "I don't know the answer," she said. "What do you want me to say?"

The unicorn stepped down from the summit of the pyramid, and Finn hid behind Gaius. "How does the world appear to you? At its most basic level, is the universe made out of order or chaos? Are there patterns or anarchy?"

There must be patterns, she thought. That's the right answer, isn't it? Good and evil; order and chaos—Gaius had mentioned those things too. *What am I supposed to say?*

The unicorn waited.

Jane said, "The universe—"

Wait. *She knew my grandmother. This thing—this Keeper or unicorn is here to stop people from hurting her home, Hotland. That's what Gaius said, right? The Keeper is afraid of me. There isn't a real answer, is there? It wants my answer so it has a better idea of who I am and whether or not I am a threat. So which is more dangerous: a person who believes there is a pattern or someone who thinks everything is random? Someone who believes in a pattern might have more of a reason to think Hotland shouldn't be real. I don't even know if I believe it. But if everything is chaos, Hotland can exist, right? If the world is crazy anyway, a talking unicorn doesn't hurt anything.*

Jane said, "The universe is chaos."

Oh, no! she thought. *What if that was the wrong answer...?*

The unicorn said, "You may all enter freely." She went back to the top of the pyramid, and a doorway opened on the opposite wall, past statues frozen in mid-stride. "I will not see you again."

Gaius clicked his tongue. "Come on."

Jane followed Gaius and Finn around the statues and into another dark corridor. Behind them, the unicorn was gone.

When an antique elevator came into view at the end of the hall, Jane asked Gaius, "Why didn't you tell me she would ask those questions? Why did she ask *me?*"

"I'm sorry, Jane," Gaius said, and the way he lingered meant that he was lying. "I don't know."

CHAPTER 12

The Way Down

As it descended, the brass and iron elevator rattled like dice in a washing machine. The walls and ceiling were inlaid with Victorian curls and hooks of polished ivory and copper; the designs reminded Jane of the ornate balconies and latticework she'd seen on a trip to New Orleans two years ago. At the time, Michael had barely noticed the French Quarter, a pair of guidebooks clutched to his chest. Ghosts. He had been obsessed with seeing ghosts, Jane remembered. Unfortunately, all the ghosts had been on vacation too.

The elevator banged and shook, and as they continued to drop, the gas lamp on the ceiling sputtered and dimmed until the white-blue flame cast only modest, upside-down shadows.

"Is this safe?" Jane said.

Gaius watched the dented iron door. "Good question. It could probably do with some repairs."

The gas lamp flicked out.

"What's wrong with the light?" Jane asked.

Gaius said, "We are crossing over."

The elevator was dark. She listened to the pounding thumps of their descent, felt each jolt in her teeth, and thought, *If I could face the unicorn, I can handle an elevator ride—even an uncomfortable, dangerous elevator ride.*

"There's nothing to be afraid of," Jane murmured.

A new voice said, "Not yet, *amiga*, but there will be."

"Who said that?"

The elevator stopped, and the light came on—lots of them. The brass and iron elevator had grown to the size of a gymnasium. The high ceiling was crowded with electric floodlights. A giant lizard with wings was watching her with red-black eyes. Green scales flowed along its flanks and ridged spine—sparkling purple and yellow on its belly. The dinosaur's hind legs were thick with muscle; its front legs were longer and ended in five-fingered claws, each as long as Jane's arm. Its head was as big as a car. The dinosaur sat up, its great wings fluttering in curls of translucent skin. She could see the joints of the bones inside—like a bat's wings.

A cat dressed in a brown robe adjusted his cane and said, "There is no need to frighten her, Finn."

Jane forced herself to look away from the dinosaur to the cat-man. The cat's gray-black fur was striped like a tabby, and when she noticed his cane—Gaius's cane—the cat-man nodded. His eyes were hazy white.

Jane shook her head. "Am I…are you…?"

"This is not a dream," the cat-Gaius said as he started for a huge sliding door. "And we should get moving."

"You're a cat!" Jane said. "I mean, how can you be a cat? I don't—"

"We are in Hotland now." Gaius continued to the door. "It's best if you stop thinking like that."

Jane said, "Finn, you're not a dog—you're some kind of giant lizard, like a dinosaur!"

The dinosaur chuckled with a low rumbling of its rib cage, like distant thunder. Gaius unhooked the heavy door, and Finn dropped back to all fours. When he spoke, she saw fangs the size of bowling pins.

"They're filling your head with oatmeal at that school," Finn said. "A *dinosaur?* Don't you know dinosaurs are extinct?"

"If you're not a dinosaur, then what are you?"

"What do you think? I'm a dragon."

Jane said, "I thought dragons weren't real."

"If we aren't real, then we aren't extinct either, are we?"

Gaius slid open the door, and Jane stared, for the first time, at Hotland—the land at the center of the world.

CHAPTER 13

Hotland

Jane said, "Wow."

The door opened from the side of a slate mountain to—animals. Lots and lots of animals. *There are too many,* Jane thought. *This is impossible.* A herd of wheat-colored antelope loitered beside a crowd of lions, ostriches, and sharp-horned rhinos, and a pack of rats mingled with clumps of pink-butt monkeys and disinterested gorillas. And birds—everywhere, there were birds. The constantly moving, constantly talking animals stood on rolling grass fields (Jane assumed it was grass; she couldn't see with all the animals in the way) that stretched to the horizon. As Jane stared, a flock of silver birds burst into the sky. She froze. Wait a second. *Talking?*

She listened. All the millions of animals (and yes, there had to be *at least* millions of them) were arguing, joking, complaining in perfect English. Finn stretched as he stepped out of the elevator, his toes and the joints in his great dragon tail popping like oversized knuckles. A group of grizzly bears scattered, calling, "Lizard! Giant lizard!" When Finn laughed, Jane felt the rumble in her own rib cage.

"*Dra-gon,*" Finn said.

The nearby animals had retreated from the elevator doors in a wide semicircle, and their animal voices were low under the rumble of conversation across the fields. The mountain behind Jane rose higher than she could see—through the clouds—and it extended like a wall in both directions. As she watched flocks of birds swoop and weave overhead, Jane murmured, "Huh." Beyond the clouds, the sky was brown, not blue. But there, above the multitudes of animals, was the sun, just like normal.

A gray furball was darting through the animals toward them.

"We need to keep moving," Gaius said, "if we hope to reach the Purple Marsh before dark."

"The Purple Marsh?" Jane said.

Gaius pointed his cane over the animals. "That way."

"What is it?" Jane said. "You haven't told me where we are— why are all these animals here? What is this place?" *And why am I speaking so quickly?* she thought. I'm shouting at him—at a talking cat! "I'm sorry, I just—"

The furball pushed out of the animal crowd and stood on its hind legs, a tiny red megaphone in one of its paws. "Who," it shouted through the megaphone, "do you think you are? And what is the meaning of this—arriving on the elevator unannounced? There are signatures required for the preliminary paperwork! I don't expect you considered where you would stay once you got here, hmm?" Its beady eyes squinted first at Finn, then at Gaius and Jane. It was some kind of groundhog, about the size of a fat toaster. "No? I thought not!" the groundhog continued. "The Sunburn Road is overcrowded as it is. I hope *you* don't expect"—and here it wrinkled its nose at Finn—"to find a comfy mattress and a piping fireplace waiting for you with no notice!"

"Actually," Gaius said, "that is exactly what we expect to find."

The groundhog blinked as if Gaius had flashed a laser pointer in its eye. "Wha-wha—*who* are you?" The nearby animals were quiet now, watching Gaius.

"My name is Gaius Saebius Marcellus."

"Gaius…?" The groundhog's jaw quivered, and it clicked the megaphone uncomfortably. "You're not the one who lives in the, uh—in the Purple…"

"Yes."

"Ah." The groundhog was clicking the megaphone frantically now, its teeth nibbling at the air "We *are* pressed for space, you understand. I am so sorry, sir…"

"I understand," Gaius said. "We will be staying in my home."

At that, the groundhog's tiny shoulders relaxed. "Of course, of course! A bobbin—silly me! I should have recognized you, but I've never met a—"

Finn farted a mushroom cloud of fire and smoke. The animals gasped, the groundhog ran back into the crowd, and Jane laughed.

"There, now," Finn said. "I feel better."

"That wasn't necessary," Gaius said.

Finn clicked his jaw. "You want it to come out the front? Climb aboard, everyone."

"Not here," Gaius said. "The sky is too crowded."

Finn looked at the birds overhead and snorted. "So? I'm bigger than them."

"No. We walk now."

"It would be much faster—"

"I said no, Finn." Gaius nodded to the animals. "But you *can* clear us a path…"

As Finn approached the animals, Jane thought, *There is something bad in this place. I don't know what, but something here is wrong, like an invisible illness.*

Gaius nodded to Jane, as if to say "Thank you," and they followed Finn onto a road of overgrown cobblestones.

CHAPTER 14

The Kangaroo

The animals may have cleared the road for Finn, but they were more interested in Gaius. As Gaius passed, there were hushed murmurs from peacocks and scrawny dogs, and Jane thought she heard a crocodile whisper "Bobbin."

"Why are they staring?" Jane asked.

"Our line leader," Gaius said, "happens to be a dragon."

He's lying again, Jane thought. *What if I can't trust him?*

"What's a *bobbin?*" she asked out loud.

"I am," Gaius said. "That's what I am called."

"Bobbins were cat-people," Finn called over his shoulder.

"Were?" Jane asked.

Gaius waved his cane at Finn. "Who knows why he says anything? He's just a stubborn dragon. No more talking. We have a long way to go."

A kangaroo bounced to Jane's side, and every time she took a step, the kangaroo hopped to catch up. Her belly pouch bulged, and she was smiling.

"Heard from Iz?" the kangaroo asked with a thick, Australian accent. The sound reminded Jane of the voice in a beer commercial that her father liked.

Jane stopped, but the others didn't notice and kept walking. "My iguana?" she asked.

The kangaroo patted her belly, and a muffled voice—from inside the pouch—said, "Jane! You have to—"

Animals wandered onto the cobblestones again, cutting off Jane from Gaius and Finn. *I have to go,* she thought. She pointed at the kangaroo's pouch. "What's in there?"

"What—*this?*" The kangaroo pulled Iz out by his tail.

"Jane!" Iz shouted. His voice was deep. "Run! He's—"

The kangaroo covered Iz's mouth with one hand. Now there were animals everywhere, mixing and chatting and clogging her path. Ahead of her, Jane spotted Finn over the herds, thirty feet away.

"Finn!" Jane called. "Gaius! Wait!"

But the animals were too loud.

"I'll make you a deal," the kangaroo said. "I'll let your friend go if you come with me."

As Jane reached for Iz, the kangaroo hopped away. Jane shouldered through a pack of llamas. When she put her foot down, something squeaked, so she jumped backward, tripped, and fell. She banged her elbow hard on the cobblestones, and for just a moment, when her head was close to the ground, she thought she heard voices singing in another language. It was a strange, jolting song, like the music from a Japanese play her mother had made her watch when Jane was in third grade. It had been full of men and women with exaggerated masks, and Jane had had nightmares for weeks afterward. *The grass,* Jane thought distantly. *The grass is singing.*

"Is it a deal?" the kangaroo said.

"Why do you want me to come with you?" Jane said. "Who are you?" She looked around, but now, there was no sign of Finn or anyone else. "Gaius!" she called.

"Look, I'm trying to be nice," the kangaroo said. "I could always break your knees and put you in my pouch, you know."

The kangaroo was a foot shorter than Jane, but its hind legs were thick muscle, and there were sharp nails on its front paws.

This isn't real, Jane told herself. *I must be asleep.* But her pulse wouldn't slow down. "If I come with you," Jane said, "you'll let Iz go?"

"That's right. What do you say?"

"Where are you going to take me?"

"To him," the kangaroo said, as if it were obvious.

"Him," Jane repeated.

"Sure. Do we have a deal, then?"

"Yes," Jane said. "But you have to let Iz go first."

The kangaroo dropped Iz, and the iguana hit the ground running.

"Run, Jane!" he shouted. "They'll kill you!"

"Ah, go on," the kangaroo told Iz, "before I stomp on you. Now, then." She looked up at Jane again. "If you'll follow me…"

Jane ran.

CHAPTER 15

Applepatch Mary

Jane twisted through a group of smelly horses and caught her balance on a broken stone wall that was covered with vines and moss. The kangaroo bounded after her. She jumped over a line of baby ducks, pushed through a herd of deer—"Excuse *me!*" one shouted—and then slid through the legs of a giant polar bear, who exclaimed, "Did you see someone just fly between my—?" when the kangaroo collided with it. The polar bear loomed over the kangaroo. Jane dodged a hippopotamus, still running.

"Sorry, mate," the kangaroo stammered, "I just have to—"

Jane hurried along another crumbling wall, past a pack of wolves, and when she looked back, the polar bear was sniffing the kangaroo's ears.

"…almost tropical," the polar bear was saying. "You're telling me this shampoo keeps the flies away twenty-four/seven, huh?"

Glaring at Jane, the kangaroo said to the polar bear, "Sure does. My sister has the recipe. Shall I have her call you?"

Jane stopped: a tumbledown stone wall opened to a grove of short, leafy trees. Although the animals were crowded around the edges of the wall, there were no animals inside the grove. It was as if the trees were off-limits. *I wonder why,* Jane thought, and she went in. If this were dangerous, it wouldn't feel so peaceful, would it?

Something squished and broke under her shoe: an apple. This was an orchard. The ground was hard, and when she scuffed the grass with her foot, a clod of dirt came away, exposing white stone. *This whole area was a city or something once,* Jane thought.

She tested the branches of the nearest apple tree; they seemed strong enough. *I'll have a better chance of spotting Finn from a higher lookout,* she thought, but when she started to pull herself up, someone groaned. Jane stumbled back. The tree shook, and an apple fell.

"That's impolite," the tree said. Its voice was a rustle, as if the leaves were speaking.

"I'm sorry," Jane said. "I wanted to climb up to look for my friends."

"Not to pick apples?"

"No."

"Smart girl," the tree said. *"You look like her."*

"Like who?"

The tree's leaves blurted the word. *"Her."*

Jane had the strangest feeling that the tree was pointing, and when she looked, she noticed something shiny through the grove.

"What is it?" Jane asked.

"Her," the tree said again.

I have to go, Jane thought. *The kangaroo might come back at any moment. I have to find Finn and Gaius.* But she stepped deeper between the trees to a place overrun with thorn bushes and sharp holly. *This is a bad idea—I should go back. I have to get out of here.* And then she saw it: a human outline in the overgrowth.

Jane yanked away brittle vines and pricked her thumb on a thorn, but she kept pulling and ripping away the vegetation. The leaves shook around her, although there was no wind, and Jane heard the trees say *"Cursed."* Finally, the mess broke away. Jane collapsed in the sweet-smelling leaves and apples. The ground was hard like thin carpet over wood.

It was a white marble statue of Jane—but not quite. On the statue, Jane's hair was curly, and there was a scar on her chin. The statue-Jane held a short, dangerous knife in her left hand and raised a stone apple with her right hand. She was dressed in a strange one-piece dress with a thick belt at the waist and a torn coat hanging over her shoulders.

The trees spasmed, shouting, *"Cursed! Forbidden!"*

A plaque at the base of the statue had the word *Traitor* chiseled into it. There had been other words, but whoever had carved *Traitor* had deliberately destroyed them.

Jane backed away. "Who is she?"

The trees jostled and howled, *"Forbidden!"* Something smacked the back of Jane's head, and she spun in time to duck a second apple.

"Stop it!" Jane shouted.

"Cursed!"

The trees threw more apples, and Jane staggered out of the overgrowth closer to the exit. An apple hit her shoulder, then her right leg. "Ow! Stop it!"

"Such a ruckus…" The kangaroo watched from the gap in the orchard wall. "What have you done now?"

The trees were quiet again, as if they wanted to hear the kangaroo.

"You're not supposed to be in there, you know," the kangaroo said. "You're either brave or stupid—or both. That's Mary's corner."

"Mary?"

"You know, Applepatch Mary."

"Who is she?"

"Come out, and I'll tell you all about her. Don't make me call for help. The others won't be nearly as likable as me. You had a good run..." As she spoke, the animals behind her began to clear. "And I don't want to hurt you, but I promise, if you don't come out of there now, I'll—"

With a rush of air like a train entering a tunnel, Finn landed behind the kangaroo. Gaius was on his back, and Iz was sitting on Gaius's lap. The kangaroo's ears pricked backward, but she was still facing Jane.

"Darn," the kangaroo said, and Jane wondered if she was about to cry. Her knees were trembling. "Jane, if you don't come out, I'll—"

Finn breathed a fireball over the kangaroo's head. "*You'll what?*" Finn said. "You will *what?*"

The kangaroo bounced to face the dragon. "Right," she said. "That is a legitimate question..."

"Run," Finn said, grinning fangs. "Or hop. Or whatever you do. Do it now, and tell him that you're lucky I wasn't hungry."

"Right, mate," the kangaroo said. "Fair enough then—"

"*Now!*" Finn huffed another fireball, and the kangaroo took off.

As Gaius climbed down, he told Finn, "That was overly dramatic. You know you don't eat marsupials."

"You never know," Finn said. "There's a first time for everything."

"You *could* take this a bit more seriously." Gaius stopped at the orchard wall. "Come out of there, Jane." She did, and Gaius said, "I'm disappointed. You haven't the slightest idea of where you are or what you're doing."

"Only because you haven't told me," Jane said. "Who is Applepatch Mary?"

"She tried to save the bobbins," Finn said. "But she couldn't because they had already been turned into—"

"*Finn!*" Gaius said. He frowned at Jane and said, "If your friend there"—he indicated Iz—"hadn't warned us, where would you be?"

Jane took Iz and said, "You tried to warn me back at our house, didn't you, Iz?"

"I'm just glad you're all right," Iz said. "And you're in good hands. That dinosaur is *much* bigger than me." Finn rolled his eyes, and Iz continued, "I should stay here. I'll only be in the way where you're going."

"He's right," Gaius said. "As long as the Raven King's magic hasn't crossed the Old Wall, this is the safest place for the animals."

Jane gave Iz a hug, and he said, "Bye, Jane. I'm sure you'll be the one."

She put Iz down and climbed onto Finn's back. "What did he mean that he's sure I'll be the one?"

"No more questions right now," Gaius said. "I'll explain more when you're ready."

"If she passes the tests, you mean," Finn said.

"Not another word," Gaius said. "It will be dark very soon. We'll have to wait until tomorrow to reach the Purple Marsh."

"Dark already?" Jane said. "But the sun is right there. It looks like the middle of the afternoon."

"It is not the middle of the afternoon," Gaius said. Finn extended his great wings to many "Oohs!" and "Aahs!" from the surrounding animals. "And that"—he pointed up—"is not the sun."

CHAPTER 16

Miles-and-Miles

After Finn took off, the daylight went out. One moment, Jane was perched at the edge of Finn's right shoulder, watching herds of buffalo and pink flamingos below, and the next, they were staring at blackness, as if the bathroom light had been flipped off in the middle of the night.

Jane said, "What happened?"

"It's all right," Gaius said behind her. "Your eyes will adjust."

He was right. Soon Jane could see gray and black outlines. But there was no moon.

"That's the way it is here," Finn said. "Twelve hours of light; twelve hours of darkness."

"We'll stop on the Sunburn Road," Gaius told him.

They landed on an old road made of big square blocks— the kind you might find in a pyramid. In the dark, Jane heard animal conversations all around them. She smelled dirty fur and wet feathers.

"All the animals left Earth—the surface—to come here," Jane said. "Didn't they?"

Gaius unrolled small packs that had been strapped to Finn's side. "Yes." And before she could ask, he said, "I told you, the Raven King will return to topside Earth very soon."

"Where does he live now?"

Gaius said, "Here in Hotland."

"But if he lives here already, why would the animals come here to get away from him?"

Gaius gave her a sleeping bag that smelled of dust and mothballs. "Here."

Jane said, "Is there any food?"

"What do you want?" Finn asked. "How's goat sound? I see a goat over there…"

"*Finn.*" Gaius said. "We'll have plenty to eat before the tests. Stay close tonight—don't leave the road."

"Why are you going to test me?" Jane said. "To find out if I'm strong enough to stop the Raven King?"

"Yes," Gaius said. "If the Raven King finds you, he will kill you." He did a slow cat-circle, then settled in. "Good night, Jane."

Jane rolled onto her back and stared at the blackness overhead. *I didn't think I could be scared of a kangaroo,* she thought. *I hope Michael, Mom, and Dad are okay. Everything is backward here. The sky is brown because we're underground,* she realized. *This is like a giant cave—as big as the world.* Jane thought about that, then decided she had to use the bathroom—but, of course, there were no toilets anywhere. She sat up and looked at the outlines of sleeping animals on the road and in the fields. Something about it bothered her, and it wasn't that they could talk. *The animals aren't interested in eating or normal animal-things,* she thought. *They just stand around chatting—as if they're waiting for something.* But what could these animals be waiting for?

Jane went to the edge of the road. Something tugged at her leg: a rabbit. A little brown bunny rabbit with beady eyes was looking up at her. He was wearing a stiff blue uniform with gold buttons, like something a ship's captain might wear.

"Excuse me, darlin'," the rabbit said. "My name is Miles, of Miles-and-Miles Courier Service. Can I ask your name?"

"Um—my name is Jane."

"Last name?"

"Lehman."

Miles whistled. "I thought so! Why, this is an honor, Miss Lehman—truly an honor. Can I shake your hand? It will be something to tell my grandkids about someday. That *I* made the delivery!"

Jane crouched to shake the rabbit's tiny paw with one finger.

"Delighted!" Miles said. "Simply delighted!"

"I'm sorry," Jane said. "I don't really understand what this is all about…"

"Why, yes, of course! Silly me!" Miles disappeared into a hole and popped out again with a piece of yellow paper and a line of string. "If you could sign here at the bottom and initial there, on the side, you can have it right now!"

Jane squinted at the paper. It was much too dark to read. "What delivery? How could you possibly know to deliver something to me?"

Miles looked hurt. "For eleven generations, we have kept…" He sniffed and started again. "Once upon a time, my great-great-great-great-great-great—"

"You have something for me that someone gave to your family a long time ago?" Jane said.

"Why, yes," Miles said, brightening. "We are the best family courier service along the Sunburn Road, bar none. Miles-and-Miles for all your needs. Which reminds me, do you have a parcel to send?"

"Um, no."

"We had explicit instructions to check this road every day for years and years until we found a girl who looked just like the girl who sent the original package. Just like you."

"Who was that?" Jane asked. "Who sent it?"

"Why, the last savior of Hotland, of course. Diana Starlight."

Grandma Diana, Jane thought. "I'll sign."

He handed her a tiny pencil, like the kind used to keep score at a miniature golf course. She scribbled her name and initials.

Miles took the paper and gave Jane the end of the string. "It's all yours, darlin'."

"It's...what do I do?"

Miles giggled. "Why, you pull. What else would you do?"

She tugged, and more of the string came out of the hole. Jane pulled harder. The string kept coming. Behind her, everyone else was still asleep on the road.

Miles said, "That's it!"

More string and more, and finally, an old envelope popped out of the hole. The cursive handwriting on the back of the envelope sparkled like the glow-in-the-dark star stickers Jane had stuck on her ceiling when she was little. It said:

Three Spells Inside,
One for Fire, One for Escape,
And One to Make the Evil One Break.

Jane opened the envelope. Inside, there were three blank slips of paper.

"But there's nothing written on these," she said.

"No, there wouldn't be yet," Miles said. "Not until you need them. I'm off then. It's been a pleasure, Miss Lehman. Truly a pleasure." He shook Jane's finger again and disappeared into the hole.

Jane stuffed the envelope and blank pages into her pocket and climbed back into her sleeping bag. *What kind of screwy present is this?* she wondered. A little poem and three blank papers—*Thanks a lot, Grandma. Very helpful.*

CHAPTER 17

The Purple Marsh

"Everybody up!" Finn called. "Up, up!"

Jane wiped her eyes. Her back and neck were sore, and she shielded her face from the light. "What time is it?" she asked. They were still surrounded by animals. Nothing had changed overnight.

"It's time to wake up," Gaius said. "Sleep well?"

Finn yawned dramatically. "Like a log."

"I wasn't asking you—I *know* you slept well." Gaius collected the sleeping bags. "Let's get ready to go. We'll eat when we get there."

When everything was packed, they climbed onto Finn's back. He jumped into the air, his wings beating—and they were off. Jane tried to watch the crowded fields pass below; she tried to think about anything but the envelope in her pocket. It didn't work.

They flew for a long time. When the Sunburn Road disappeared behind them, clumps of gray and green trees broke up the grassland. There were fewer animals. Soon the ground sloped away, the vegetation thickened into a swamp of vines and tangled canopy, and Finn landed at the edge. Ahead the mud became brackish water crusted red, as if it were rusted. Inside the bog, where the trees and bushes thickened, the air was dark, humid, and red. It smelled of rotten wood and mud.

"Why do they call it the Purple Marsh?" Jane asked. "It's not purple."

"It *was* purple a long time ago," Gaius said.

Finn went to the edge of the embankment and sighed. "I hate this part. Well? Everybody ready?" When they were secure on Finn's back, he slid into the water. It rose to his belly, just below the sleeping bags. When Finn waded deeper, the red surface rippled, and Jane could see that the brown water below was full of the shadows of fish. Finn swam between mud-islands, ugly trees, and moldering logs. Bird-voices cawed overhead, and there was the constant drone of insect voices, rhythmic and indistinct. Jane couldn't make out the words.

Finn stopped at a bank of reddish muck. "Here we are," he said.

"Stay here, Jane," Gaius said, and Finn helped Gaius to the muddy shore. The ground squished and oozed when Gaius walked with his cane. "Sandra?" he called. "Sandra, darling?"

The insects and birds quieted.

Gaius rapped his cane on a tree. "Sandra? Come out, please—we are in a hurry, darling."

Jane whispered, "Who's Sandra?"

"Guardian of the marsh," Finn said. "This is her land. She only lets Gaius live here because she has a crush on him." Gaius frowned back, and Finn said, "What? It's true."

"Why does he need to find her?"

"Unless Sandra gives permission, there is no way through. We'd get lost in here. And wouldn't that be inconvenient?"

"*There* you are!" a woman's voice said. "My dear Gaius Saebius, you look thin. How are you?"

Jane squinted at the mud where Gaius was smiling, but there was no one there.

"Busy as always, darling," Gaius said. "And you?"

"The Raven King's magic crossed the Old Wall this morning."

Gaius stopped smiling. "Are you sure?"

"Yes, I'm afraid so, dear."

Now Jane saw it: a red frog squatted in the mud, camouflaged perfectly except for her lips, which were painted just a bit too pink. She seemed to be wearing eyeliner.

"I'm so sorry, Gaius," the frog—Sandra—said. "You are almost out of time. You know, we're all counting on you to find the one. I know you will."

"Thank you," Gaius said. "How is the family?"

"*Don't* ask," Sandra said. "Honestly." She croaked a laugh. "*You* get those children sorted out. But first, give me a kiss."

"Of course," Gaius said. He knelt and planted a kiss on Sandra's lips. When he stood, there was frog-lipstick all over his whiskers.

"And here you go," Sandra said. "Candles to light your way." Glowing red orbs appeared in the marsh ahead. They were decorated with black strips and Chinese characters.

"Thanks again, darling," Gaius said as he returned to Finn.

"Not at all," Sandra said. "You just be careful! Something is coming."

"I will," Gaius called, and he blew another kiss.

When they passed the first light, Jane smiled. "Sandra likes you, Gaius."

Gaius's fur prickled, like a cat blushing. "Sandra is very old and wise."

"You two—"

Finn cleared his throat, interrupting her.

They were quiet until they stopped at the last light. Behind them, the swamp was dark again: the orbs were gone. *We couldn't leave now even if we wanted to,* Jane thought. As they climbed onto the mud, she thought, *There's nothing here.*

Gaius pointed at the swamp and said, "Reveal."

The castle revealed itself.

CHAPTER 18

The Hidden Tree

It didn't pop out of the swamp, and it certainly did not magically appear. Instead the air shifted and slouched, as if Jane were watching invisible curtains being drawn aside. First she saw the middle, then the sides. It was a castle, certainly; but it was also a tree. The castle rose to three towers that she could see—two at the corners and the largest in the center—although Jane imagined there might be third and fourth corner towers at the rear (and she was right). The tops of the walls were ridged—for lookouts, she assumed—and irregular windows of stained glass dotted the sides above a heavy iron door.

Leaves grew from the walls, and bizarre branches sprouted from the tops of the towers. At first glance, it was a traditional castle—with unorthodox windows and branches but *still* a castle—but the longer Jane examined it, the more tree features she found. The base was stumped with roots, and the surface was rough bark, not stone; this was *not* a tree that had been chopped down. No, this giant tree had grown a door-hole, windows, towers—even the serrated lookout points—and, Jane assumed (again rightly), a hollow interior so people, or bobbins, could live inside.

As he followed Gaius, Finn said, "There's bird poop on the twelfth king."

Jane followed Finn's gaze to bobbin statues built—no, *grown*—into the castle wall, each as tall as a house. The bobbins wore robes and armor, and their faces were grim, like the expressions of television soldiers or tennis players…if they let giant cat-people play tennis. Finn was right: the closest bobbin relief had a white smear on his cat nose and eyes.

"Thanks, girls," Finn called to the trees, and Jane saw segmented legs move in the branches. She glimpsed a face with eight black eyes above a pincer mouth.

"Welcome home," the spider murmured, followed by a cacophony of "—elcome home." "—home."

The air behind them changed. Jane couldn't describe what happened: she *smelled* something move. *A spider web*, she thought. *It was hiding the castle when we first approached. It opened to let us through, and now it has shut again.* It made her uneasy. *No one out there can see us,* Jane realized. *We're invisible.*

"It's so hidden," Jane said.

"That's right," Finn said. "The only people who can find the castle are people who have been here before."

Although it had looked impressive from the distance, as they neared the iron entry door, Jane felt uneasy. How could a tree grow into this shape, she wondered, with windows and bobbin statues in its bark? It didn't seem natural.

Someone laughed from the top of the wall, and when Jane looked up, she saw a flash of red, like a hat or a coat. "Are there other kids here?" she asked.

"Yes," Gaius said.

"Why?"

When Gaius reached the front door, he said, "You'll find out shortly." He rapped, a lock clicked, and the door opened. "Welcome to Castle Alsod, my home."

CHAPTER 19

Introductions

Inside, the tree wasn't a tree. Instead of the roots and tree rings and sap smell Jane had expected, they entered a great hall of gears. Beneath the floor and in the walls—all the way up to the giant ceiling—round gears clicked and clacked, tapped and tocked, as if they had stepped into the dream of a giant clock. There were silver gears and red gears, wooden gears and dark granite gears, all crammed into a complicated network of moving, murmuring parts. *It's glass,* Jane realized. The floor, the walls, and the ceiling were all transparent glass with the gears on the other side.

Jane said, "Why does it look like a tree from the outside?"

Finn ducked and squeezed. Jane was certain he wouldn't fit through the entryway, until the doorway yawned around Finn and the dragon slipped inside. The doorway shrank again.

"A tree is never just a tree," Gaius said. "This is *not* a tree. This is Castle Alsod. And we're late."

Something the size of a big bumblebee zipped from the far end of the hall to Gaius. It had a long skinny nose, and its wings whirred too quickly to see. Its segmented body clicked each time it jerked from one side of Gaius's face to the other. *A humming-bird,* Jane thought, and she tried to get a better look. Finn was picking his nose. It seemed to be a wooden hummingbird with a click-clack body like a toy and bright blue eyes. It was wearing a pointy maroon hat and matching sweater.

The hummingbird chirped, "Lord of the manor, last of your noble race and guardian—"

"Just Gaius," Gaius said.

"Oh, noble Just-Gaius—"

"Mallory, you can call me Gaius, remember?" Gaius said. "Nothing else."

"Yes, lord," Mallory the wooden hummingbird said. "They are assembled in the dining hall."

"All of them?"

Mallory fluttered neurotically and said, "Um, yes, I believe we have collected—"

"*All* of them?" Gaius asked again.

"Sire, there is one unaccounted for—it wasn't my fault! He must have heard the meal bell, but we've looked everywhere! My lord, if anyone is to be punished, I beg that you take my life and spare the kitchen staff! Surely, I am to—"

"He is on the roof," Gaius said, and they walked toward a set of brass doors at the end of the hall.

"Of course!" Mallory said. "Your magical powers are stronger than anything your humble servants might—"

"I heard him when we came up the front walk," Gaius said. "Please go tell him it's time to eat." Mallory left, and Gaius said, "Jane, I hope you're hungry."

The doors opened on a marble banquet hall of long tables full of a hundred laughing, shouting children. Jane's stomach clenched. It was just like the cafeteria at school; everyone had a seat except her. *It's all right,* she thought. *I'll slip around the back wall and look for an empty place where no one will notice me. I can blend in and pretend that I've been here all along...*

Finn shot a fireball over the center of the hall, and Gaius shouted, "*Attention!*" The room went quiet, and hundreds of eyes were watching Jane, waiting. Her mouth was dry. She felt sick. "All of you are here because you have potential," Gaius said, "but *this* is Jane!" Jane felt heat in her cheeks, and Gaius continued, "Her family was saving the world before you or your parents or your great-great-great grandparents were in diapers! She is the first, best hope in this room!"

A tall boy slipped through a side door with Mallory buzzing at his ear. The boy was tan with a shock of short dark hair. He crossed his arms when he saw Jane, unimpressed. He wore a red jacket.

"Jane is the one we have been waiting for, and tomorrow, the tests will begin! But now," Gaius said, "let's eat!"

CHAPTER 20

Meal Time

Everyone started talking and shouting and laughing again.

"Dinner today is roast monkey liver," Gaius said, "in a white wine garlic sauce."

Jane paled. "Oh."

"I'm only joking," Gaius said. "Go sit down. When we're finished, Finn will show you to your room."

Mallory flew to Gaius and said, "My lord and master, we have a message from the Great Falls…"

Gaius nodded and went with the hummingbird and Finn, leaving Jane alone.

As she walked around the edge of the tables, children stared. Most wore ordinary shirts and jeans or school uniforms or bulky jackets, but there were also groups dressed in bright robes and turbans, and even several girls wearing black, face-covering veils, like the images of people from desert countries in *National Geographic*. Jane heard German and French and sing-song Asian languages being spoken, but most of all, she heard English. Most of the kids seemed to speak English.

Just stay calm, she told herself. *I'll find a place to sit. I have to blend in—*

Jane ran into a giant, wooden, mechanical crab carrying trays of food. The crab was as large as a trash can, and when she collided with it, plates, saucers, glasses, silverware, and napkins went flying in every direction in a tremendous clattering, crashing smash that made everyone fall silent again. The crab's green eyes looked from one end of the mess to the other as it struggled to balance one last glass of milk atop its front claw—and the glass fell, exploding in glittery chips and milk on the floor.

"Oh, dear," the crab said.

"Nice job, savior!" someone called, and the room erupted into laughter.

Jane murmured an apology and stumbled away, her face bright red. She went to a far table that was completely empty except for one Indian girl dressed in an *I ♥ NY* T-shirt reading a thick book. She blinked when Jane sat.

"I'm sorry," the girl said in a vaguely British accent. "Would you like me to move?"

"No, it's okay," Jane said. "I mean, you can if you want to, but I don't mind. You don't have to move for me."

"Okay," the girl said, and she went back to reading her book.

Boys at a nearby table were looking at Jane and laughing, but Jane told herself she didn't care—except that she wanted to crawl into a corner and cry. *Why does it always have to happen like this?* she thought. *Why can't I do anything right?*

The tall dark-haired boy in the red jacket came to stand behind a chair across from Jane. Ignoring the Indian girl, he studied Jane as if she were a four-leaf clover or an Olympic medal—something rare that he knew he should respect but didn't.

"So you're here to save us from the Raven King?" the boy said.

He was a few years older than Jane, maybe fifteen or sixteen, and he was American.

"I don't know," Jane said. "No. I don't think so."

"Are you going to throw plates and spoons at him?"

Without looking up, the Indian girl said, "Give it a rest, Thomas."

"It's a fair question," Thomas said. "Gaius said she's the one, didn't he?"

"Gaius doesn't know," the girl said. "No one does." She smiled at Thomas. "Now please go away. I can't read with you talking."

She pronounced *can't* as *cahn't*.

"I don't care who your family was," Thomas told Jane. "You don't belong here."

"Says the boy who's late to every meal," the Indian girl said.

"Shut up, Manali." Thomas looked like he wanted to say something else, but Jane sank low in her chair, eyes down, so he finally cleared his throat and left.

"Sorry about that," Manali said. She set down her book and offered Jane a hand to shake. "I'm Manali. I'm from Mumbai."

"You're from India?" Jane shook her hand. "Wow, it must be so interesting to live there."

"It's okay," Manali said. "You're American? My aunt is American, from New Jersey. I've only been there twice, and both times I got sick. Do people there really watch American football instead of ordinary football—you call it *soccer*, yeah?"

"Yes, that's right. I mean, yes, we do."

"Is it true what Gaius said—that your mother or someone saved the world?"

"I don't know," Jane said. "I guess she might have—not my mother but maybe my grandmother. Who was that boy?"

"Thomas? Oh, he's older—you know how older boys are, yeah?" She smiled, as if they were sharing a private joke. "Their bodies are growing too fast for their brains."

"I didn't want to come here," Jane said. "But my grandmother…" She was suddenly about to cry and stopped herself. Everything was happening so quickly, as if Jane had accidentally slipped into a marathon without a chance to catch her breath.

Manali patted Jane's hand. "It'll be all right. One of these kids will be strong enough to stop him—maybe you; maybe someone else. Gaius will figure out which one of us it is, and everything will be okay."

"The Raven King? What are we supposed to do—I don't even know who he is."

"I wouldn't worry about it right now. He's a bad guy—like in a storybook, yeah?—and the bad guys always lose at the end. That's how the world works, isn't it?"

Manali said *innit* instead of *isn't it*.

A mechanical crab brought two covered plates of food. The first, for Manali, was a spicy red sauce of potatoes and chicken cubes over white rice with slices of warm flatbread on the side.

"Wow," Jane said. "What is that?"

"Chicken vindaloo," Manali said. "My favorite."

Well, Jane thought, *I've never tried it, but it* does *smell good, and*

I guess I could eat it... The second plate was a row of three chicken tacos with white cheese, refried beans, Mexican rice, a basket of warm salted chips, salsa, and chili con queso.

This time Manali said, "Cool—that looks good."

"I love chicken tacos," Jane said, amazed.

Each child received a different meal. Wooden crabs brought hamburgers and french fries, waffles, goat and rice skewers, soups, lobster, and plates of elaborate, colorful piles that Jane had never seen before that smelled like citrus or almonds or beef—all wonderful.

When Jane reached for a chip, Manali offered her a piece of flatbread and said, "Naan?"

"It's called naan?"

"That's the bread, yes," Manali said. "I'll give you some naan if I can try your chips."

"Okay, but only if you'll take a taco for some chicken vinder."

"*Vindaloo*," Manali said and smiled. "It's a deal. But you'll definitely need lots of water."

Maybe—just maybe—Jane thought, this wouldn't be so bad after all.

CHAPTER 21

Thomas

After Jane had finished eating, she said good night to Manali. "I'll see you for breakfast, yeah?" Manali said. "And call for me if anyone gives you a hard time again." Then Jane wandered out one of the many, many side doors at the back of the room to look for a bathroom. It opened to a corridor of white-veined black marble. Bobbin masks—Jane thought they looked like wax casts—were mounted on either side, flickering with yellow-orange candlelight. But there were no candles behind them. No doors either, and the corridor grew dark in the distance.

Wrong way, Jane thought, but when she turned to go, someone cleared his throat. Thomas was leaning against the wall, his arms crossed.

"I'm sorry," Jane stammered. "I shouldn't…"

"Be here?" Thomas said, and he stepped closer. "Who was it in your family? Who was so special?" When Jane went for the door, he said, "Are you afraid? It's a simple question: Who in your—?"

"My grandmother," Jane said. "And other women before her. What about you?"

"Me?" Thomas shrugged, as if that didn't matter. "Do you think I was given anything? You have an easy life, I can tell. You want to help your family—good for you. My dad is dead now because of"—he gestured at the walls and ceiling—"all of this."

"What are you talking about?"

"You're just a kid," Thomas said, and he came closer, his hands balled to fists. "How old are you—ten, eleven?"

"I'm twelve."

"I'm sixteen, and my family—you know what? I don't have to explain anything to you." When she stared back, he smirked. "You want to know, huh? He saved Gaius. When I was a baby, my dad died to save Gaius's life."

"I didn't know the Raven King—"

"Not from the Raven King; it was something else. If you tell anyone…"

"I won't."

"I don't care if we're from the same place, Jane. You and I are nothing alike." He was breathing fast, his arms tense, ready to hit her. "Stay away from me."

"Okay."

Something *bonged* behind the door, and Jane opened it again. Gaius was banging a gold gong, like something from the Forbidden Palace or the Great Wall of China, Jane imagined. "Children?" Gaius waited, but the kids kept talking. "Everyone, please…"

Thomas slipped in beside Jane. "Hey!" he shouted. "*Listen!*"

The room went silent, and Gaius smiled. "Thank you, Thomas. Dinner is over, children, and you all have a long day tomorrow. To your rooms. Scoot, scoot!"

"There," Finn said to Jane, "how was it?"

"The food? Great."

A side door grew large enough for Finn, and she followed the dragon up a red-marble staircase.

"Was I the last one to get here?" Jane asked.

"Yes," Finn said. "There was a hiding spell around your family. Gaius didn't think he would ever find you, but then someone else broke the spell."

"You mean the Raven King?"

Finn was quiet. They continued up, passing a closed wooden door with a cartoon-bobbin painted on it in bright red and blue.

"Most of Castle Alsod is off-limits," Finn said. "It's not safe to wander off without me or Gaius with you."

He didn't answer me, Jane thought, *so I'm probably right: The Raven King, whoever he is, found us—found Grandma Diana. She must have cast the spell in the first place.*

"Finn, do you know anything about Thomas?"

"Why, did he say something to you?"

She shook her head. "Never mind." They passed another door with a picture of a raindrop on it. Jane asked, "How come the castle doors open wide for you?"

"She likes me."

"Who does?"

"Alsod."

"I thought Alsod was the name of the castle."

"It is," Finn said. "And she likes me."

"How can a castle be a person?" Jane asked.

"She isn't a person; she's a castle."

"But you're talking about her—it—like a person."

"Jane, this is Hotland. I'm a talking dragon, remember?" Finn smiled. "Alsod has been the home of bobbins—the cat-people like Gaius—for thousands of years."

But there aren't any other bobbins besides Gaius, Jane thought. They stopped at a third door with a picture of two open hands on it. The stairs continued up and up and up. *Strange that this door has human hands on it,* Jane thought, *if this is a bobbin castle.*

"Here we are," Finn said. He opened the door. On the other side was a hall made of blue brick. Fireflies blinked and winked in a cloud near the ceiling, and in the yellowish glow, Jane saw pairs of unmarked doors that disappeared into darkness down the hall. "This is your floor," Finn said. "The room on the left is for you, Jane. Alsod is dangerous in the dark. Trust me."

Jane went to her door. "Where is everyone else?"

"On other floors."

"What if I have to go to the bathroom?"

"The bathroom is attached to your room, just like in a hotel." Now, lights out is in fifteen minutes," Finn nodded to the fireflies, "so hurry to bed, kiddo."

CHAPTER 22

The Fall of the Raven King

Finn said, "Here, let me get you settled into your room…"

The room was red and plushy, with shiny brass at the edges of the tables and chairs—like it was some kind of archaic parlor, rather than a bedroom—although there *was* a high, puffy bed.

"Ta-da!" Finn said. When Jane didn't smile, he walked her to the bed. "I bet you're tired, huh?"

"I don't understand any of this," Jane said. "Please, Finn. I need you to tell me why I'm here. Who is the Raven King?"

"He's…it's not…" Finn sighed and sat at the foot of the bed. "Get comfortable, *amiga*. Gaius thinks it's better not to scare you, but I guess explaining things can't hurt, can it? Are you sure you want to know? Okay…a long time ago, when the Earth was young, people were watched over by Great Eagles."

"By birds?" Jane said.

"They were like birds, yes, but they were very powerful. Anyway, they protected people. I don't know where they came from, but there were twelve of them. Back then, there was no war, no starvation—none of the horrible things you read about or see on television. It was as peaceful as you can imagine—until one day, when a thirteenth eagle came. He was stronger than all twelve of the other eagles combined, and he didn't like people."

"Why not?"

"I don't know. Have you ever been around a person who is angry at you or seems to hate you for no reason?"

Jane smiled. "I've been to school."

"I'm serious," Finn said. "This is different. Maybe people could do things that he couldn't, like love or work together, but he hated them—I mean, *really* hated them. Well, the other eagles knew they couldn't fight him, so they found one person who was different than all the others—someone who was special. And they gave her a weapon called the Name of the World. They made the Name of the World invisible to the bad eagle so he couldn't see it. He still can't. Anyway, when the bad eagle attacked, this person fought back, and she beat him. She made him leave the Earth forever. So he came here to Hotland."

"But the Raven King came back," Jane said.

"Yes. He's tried to get revenge a bunch of times, but every time, there is one person who can fight him. And every time, that person has stopped him."

"What about the bobbins?"

"Before the Raven King got here, the bobbins ruled Hotland. They were good guys—real warrior-poet types."

"What happened to them?"

Finn coughed. "The Raven King got rid of them."

"All of them? What about the other good eagles?"

"The Raven King got them too," Finn said. "I told you there was a reason Gaius doesn't like to talk about this. Now into bed. Lights out."

Jane kicked off her shoes and climbed into bed. "What is the Name of the World?"

"It's the only thing that can hurt the Raven King—if the right person uses it."

"I know, but what *is* it?"

"Hey, I'm just a dragon. I don't have all the answers. Your grandmother knew—she was the last one to use it."

Jane tried not to remember the way Grandma Diana had crumpled on the couch. That's what the Raven King had been trying to find, Jane realized. That's what he had been asking Grandma Diana about: he wanted to destroy the Name of the World so nothing could hurt him.

"If Gaius thinks that I can stop the Raven King because of my family," Jane said, "then why are the other kids here?"

"Well, there's always a chance, I guess…" Finn swallowed as he went to leave. "Gaius might be wrong."

CHAPTER 23

Laughter

The next morning, Jane wiped sleep sand from her eyes and forked a waffle bite in syrup. It tasted warm and sugary and wonderful, but she couldn't concentrate. All the things Finn had told her went around and around in her head. Although she usually forgot her dreams, today was different. In her sleep, Jane had been standing at the center of a hurricane, with winds rushing in a dark vortex around her, ripping trees from the earth, shredding homes as if they were made of toothpicks, and she had heard someone laughing. It wasn't an evil laugh—not the kind of laugh a villain or a monster would make in a movie. No, this was cold laughter. It was worse than evil because whoever was laughing was causing this destruction, and he simply didn't care the way a normal person should.

She'd awakened frightened and shivering, and although Finn had consoled her, Jane couldn't shake the dream or forget the horrible things the Raven King was supposed to have done. He'd killed all the Great Eagles and all the bobbins—all but Gaius—and now he wanted to do the same thing to ordinary people everywhere.

Manali watched Jane from across the table. They sat at the same empty table in the noisy, early-morning dining hall. "You're not hungry?" Manali said. "What's wrong?"

Jane still hadn't talked with anyone about the things Finn had told her—or about Grandma Diana's envelope that the rabbit had delivered to her on the Sunburn Road.

"What's wrong?" Manali asked again.

"I'm just sleepy," Jane said. "Manali, do you ever worry that maybe he—maybe the Raven King—could find us here?"

Manali looked confused. "What are you on about?"

"What if he finds us before we're ready—before Gaius figures out which one of us is supposed to fight?"

"Silly, this castle is hidden like a Russian doll. Only someone who has been here before can find Castle Alsod, and I'm sure the Raven King has never been here." But that didn't make Jane feel any better. She was about to say more when a fireball burst in the center of the room, and Gaius called, "*Attention!*" Talking stopped, and everyone turned to listen. Gaius stood on a platform at the front of the room, beside his gong. "I hope you are all rested and ready. The tests begin today. Only one of you can face the Raven King. Today we'll discover who it is. All your families have accomplished histories of magic, but none of that matters now.

"Our enemy is moving, so let me be very clear about this. Think of everything in the world that you love. Think about your families and your friends; think about your toys and your routines; think about your favorites places, your favorite smells, and your favorite memories. If the Raven King is not stopped, all of that will be lost. I don't want to scare you, but only one of you can face him because only one of you will be clever enough and strong enough to find and use the Name of the World."

From the back of the hall, Thomas called, "Where is it?"

Kids turned to look, and Gaius said, "I don't know. Today there will be three trials. Only one of you will pass all three. Are there any questions?"

A boy at another table burped, and children laughed. But Gaius didn't.

"Let me say this again," he said more quietly than before. "If our champion fails or if none of you passes all three tests, then we are all going to die."

Thomas stared back at Gaius, unfazed.

"Now, then," Gaius said. "If you fail a test, you will be immediately disqualified, and you will go home tonight. You have only one chance to pass each test. Does everyone understand? Good. Please stand up and head for the front door in an orderly manner. The first test is to walk on water."

CHAPTER 24

Dark Water

They gathered on a plateau of dried mud alongside Castle Alsod, and Gaius said, "Before magic or skill, you need confidence. Your parents and your teachers have taught you that there is no such place as Hotland and that the Raven King is imaginary. That is completely backward. Right now the Raven King is using technology—electronic distractions like televisions, radios, computers, and phones—to muddle your parents' minds. By the time they realize that they are in danger, it will be too late. You must believe in yourself and in Hotland. You must believe," Gaius said, "that you can walk on water."

The swamp trees faded like ghosts, leaving red water as far as Jane could see. In the distance, something arched over the water like a leafless tree trunk.

"Each of you will *walk* out there," Gaius said, indicating the arch. "Finn is waiting on the other side. The Purple Marsh is home to many hungry things. Do not look at the shadows under the water. They will leave you alone if you ignore them. Does everyone understand?" He waited. "Good. Then who's first?"

Thomas pushed to the front of the group and said, "I am."

"Walk across the water," Gaius said. "Do not doubt that you can..."

"I understand," Thomas said, and he stepped onto the muck. The red water rippled in petroleum-rainbow rings, and Thomas's foot went in. He paused, closed his eyes, and stepped out. The water caught him. There were whispers and gasps as Thomas slowly walked, never pausing, closer to the arch. His outline grew murky, until finally he passed under the arch and was gone.

"You see," Gaius said. "It can be done. But before you take a step, you must *know* that you can do it."

"I'll go next," a pale boy said.

Gaius whispered in the boy's ear. The boy nodded, looked seriously at the water, took a step—and went splashing in. Children laughed, and Gaius hauled the boy out. The water left an orange stain on the boy's skin and clothes.

"I'll try harder," the boy said, wiping his face. "I just need to—"

"I'm sorry," Gaius said. "Return to your room."

"But I didn't even have a chance," the boy said. "Come on, I barely touched the water."

"I'm sorry," Gaius said again, and he motioned to the next girl. "Go ahead, Julia."

Julia made it three steps before the water gave, collapsing like a rotten board under her shoes. She swam back to the shore and climbed out, dripping and hugging her shirt. Three more kids fell in before another boy—a German named Gerhard—made it across. The losers were told to return to their rooms to dry off and get ready to go home. *Such a long way to come for nothing,* Jane thought. *It's too bad.*

She watched them fall in, one after another, until finally a third kid—a girl from Africa—made it across. Jane waited at the back of the crowd with Manali as it went on and on and on. At first the dunks elicited laughter, and when someone started to walk across, kids cheered and clapped, but now it was as monotonous as a math test. *Splash, splash, splash,* walk. *Splash,* walk, *splash, splash.*

A girl who had walked halfway to the arch lost her footing and slipped under the water. Gaius called, "Marie?" Something surfaced near the spot where she had fallen in—it looked like a shark fin—and it went under again. "Marie!" Gaius raised his stick and said, "*Aparte jumbat!*"

The air sucked out of Jane's lungs, and she gasped as a hole opened in the water—vacuumed out by the wind—where Marie had gone under. Jane could only see the top of the whirlpool. Something thrashed at the foaming edge, like a green limb with claws. Someone near Jane was crying and speaking in French. Jane could only make out the words *Marie* and *desole*, which sounded a lot like *desolate.*

Gaius lowered his staff, and the water settled again. But Marie didn't come out.

"I'm sorry, Rory," Gaius told the crying French girl. He put his arm around her. "She was almost across…"

"I don't want to," the French girl said, shaking her head at the water and the empty place where Marie had been. "No!"

"All right." Gaius held her for a long moment. "It's all right. Go back to your room."

Rory left, sobbing. Jane's hands were shaking, and her pulse was loud in both ears. *Oh no,* she thought. *What happened to that girl? Is she dead? Why couldn't Gaius bring her out?*

"Jane," Gaius said. "It's your turn."

Jane clenched her fists, and Manali patted her shoulder.

"You'll do fine," Manali murmured. "Really."

At the edge of the lake, Gaius leaned close and whispered, "You don't have to do this. You can turn around and go home. If you give up now, it will be easier for you—there will be no risk or danger."

Jane stared at him. How could he say this now? After she'd come all this way?

"What are you talking about?" Jane said.

"You can quit," he said softly, "and go home."

Jane backed away from him. "No, I can't. The Raven King hurt my grandmother," her voice was shaking, "and my parents…Stop it."

Jane stepped into the water—her shoe sank, and she pulled it back, closed her eyes. *I can do this. It's not water; this isn't the real world. I can do anything here—I am the granddaughter of Diana Starlight, and I'm not afraid of the Raven King or a stupid pond.*

She walked across the lake. The surface rippled around Jane's feet, as if her shoes were large stones someone had skipped. She kept walking closer to the arch. A fin—like a green shark fin—surfaced to her left, but she told herself to ignore it, to watch the arch. *Don't look,* she thought, *don't look at the shadows under the water. Don't think about the girl who fell in. It was right about here, wasn't it? This is how far she got.* Jane's footsteps slowed. Her legs were trembling.

I am not afraid, she told herself. *I can do this.* But Jane had stopped walking. She was standing halfway between the shore and the arch—it wasn't a tree. *What is that thing?* she wondered. Something splashed behind her. Another fin rippled on her right. Dark shapes—like organic submarines—crisscrossed underwater in front of her. *I'm standing on the water,* Jane thought. *This is impossible. I can't be standing here.* The surface began to sag, as if she were on a bubble that was about to pop. *I'm going to fall in…!*

"Come back!" Gaius shouted. "Jane!"

No. She took another step. Heart pounding, she sucked a deep breath and kept going. A fin brushed her left shoe, but she didn't look down. The arch was made of giant gray bones. It was the spine and neck of a skeletal dragon, its huge skull dipped into the water on her left, as if it were pausing for a drink. There was no sign of its arms or ribs. Finn was waiting on the other side.

"There she is!" he said, and he plucked Jane out of the water.

He dropped her carefully onto a small mudflat where the others who had walked across were waiting. Jane collapsed, and they rushed to congratulate her—all but Thomas. He stood by himself, watching the sky.

"Congratulations, Jane!" someone said.

"I knew you would make it!"

Thomas glanced at her. "I knew you would make it. I bet you were confident," he said. "I bet Marie was too."

CHAPTER 25

The Raven King's Vengeance

About forty of them made it across the water; Manali was the last one. After Finn carried them back to Castle Alsod, Gaius waved his staff: the marsh trees, vines, and mud banks faded back in, as if they'd been hidden behind fog. The rest of the kids had returned to their rooms, and as Gaius walked them to the back of the Castle, he said, "Some of you probably knew Marie. This is not a game. The next two tests will prove who has the ability to stop *him*. You all believe in yourselves. That's good—that's a start. But it isn't enough. You cannot hurt the Raven King alone. No one can…"

Wait a second, Jane thought. *I did hurt him, didn't I? When he was disguised as a boy, I slapped him, and his lip was bleeding.*

"Only the Name of the World can hurt him."

Someone murmured, "Like a comic book bad guy or something…"

Gaius frowned. "In your stories, the good hero always wins by slaying the dragon." Finn *harrumphed* and farted fire. "In reality," Gaius continued, "the Raven King is alive and well. He may have been beaten in the past, but each time he is beaten, he comes back and takes revenge. He doesn't shout or make threats, as villains do in stories. Instead he simply kills. He kills his enemies and their families and their children—everyone."

Gaius stopped behind the castle, beside a steel door in the ground—like a cellar hatch with thick locks. "I know all about this," Gaius said, "because I had a family once. Once upon a time, I was not the only bobbin in the world." He smiled sadly. "This is real, children." Gaius tapped the cellar door. "You cannot fight the Raven King without the Name of the World, and no one knows where the Name is now. Our champion must be perceptive. The second test is to find one of three keys and use it to unlock a golden door. Inside that door, you will find the third test. Only one of you will pass."

Thomas asked, "What's the third test?"

Gaius knocked on the door with his cane, and the locks unbolted. He said, "A trial by fire." The cellar door opened; below, stone steps descended into blackness. "But first you must find the needle in the haystack."

"The key in the basement, more like," Manali whispered.

"All right," Gaius said. "Everybody in." They all went to the stairs in a line; Thomas was the first one down. "If you find yourself in danger," Gaius said, "or you want to give up, call out my name, Gaius Saebius. Understand?" He patted Jane's shoulder as she followed Manali down. There were deep grooves in the center of the steps, as if a thousand generations of people had walked down them. "Good luck."

CHAPTER 26

Tunnels

At the bottom of the stairs, everyone disappeared. Even the steps were gone. Jane was alone in the darkness. As her eyes adjusted, she saw that it was an empty stone hallway with shelves of dark shapes on the walls. The light was grainy, sawdust gray.

She heard footsteps behind her. Back there the hall split into three identical paths. *So I'm not alone,* Jane thought. *Maybe we were all transported away from each other to make it harder.* She opened her mouth to call out—then shut it again. What if the footsteps weren't from one of the other children? Gaius warned that it would be dangerous. What if there were other things down here—like the fish or whatever it was in the swamp? Better to walk away from the footsteps, not toward them. So she did.

The hall turned to the right and then forked. The footsteps faded behind her. She heard the mumbled echo of voices—boys talking—and then silence again. She went left. After a long walk, she came to another two-way intersection. This time she went right. *This is a maze,* Jane thought. *We're supposed to wander around in a dark maze until three of us randomly find keys…? What kind of silly test is this? What if I'm farther from the keys than someone else? What if the keys are on one of these shelves?* She crept closer to the wall. The shapes on the shelves were too dark to see. *This is what old tombs look like,* Jane thought. *Catacombs—that's what they were called: the places where people were buried in old cities a long, long time ago. Is this a cemetery?* The thought made her shiver. *So what if it is? They're just bones.*

This is not just a tunnel, she told herself. *This isn't even topside Earth. No telling what's down here.* She leaned closer to the wall and closed her eyes as she extended her right hand. *Stop,* a part of her said. *I'll touch a chattering skull. It will bite off my fingers and…*nothing. Her hand slipped straight through the dark shapes. *There's nothing there,* Jane realized. *It's some kind of optical illusion. The shelf is a hole.*

Footsteps. Jane pulled her arm back and spun, the German boy, Gerhard, approached.

"Is this the correct direction, do you think?" he asked.

"I don't know."

"I am going to go that way, okay?"

"Okay," Jane said, and he continued down the right side of an intersection ahead. "Wait!"

He paused. "Yes?"

"Have you seen Manali?"

"No, sorry," he said. "But I heard a girl screaming. In the wall. I don't know if it was her. Okay?"

He left, and Jane steadied herself on the shelf. *Someone was screaming inside the wall,* she thought. *Maybe the shelf isn't the right way to go after all. Maybe the keys aren't in there.* She waved one hand through the dark lumps on the shelf. The hole there was narrow and skinny, like a vent, maybe eighteen inches high. That should be big enough for me to squeeze in, Jane thought. But someone in there had been screaming. What if it was Manali? Jane had to help her.

Why? another part of Jane asked. *You barely know Manali, and anyway, it probably wasn't her. Keep checking the hall-maze; that's what Gerhard was doing.* But that could go on forever, until Gaius finally announced that someone else found a key and passed the third test.

So what?

Jane swallowed. *Let someone else win. I already passed the first test; no one can say I didn't try—because I did. They'll never know that I didn't want to go any farther. Why not wait here until it's over? I'm not the right one anyway. I'm too awkward and dumb to save anyone...aren't I?*

"Jane?" Jane turned. Manali was smiling at her. "There you are! Gerhard said you were back here. I can't believe how we got separated at the start. Are you all right? You look a bit pale. Do you need to sit down?"

"No, I'm fine," Jane said.

"Great! Then how about it? Which way should we go?"

"I don't know."

"I say, left is right—of course, if we do that enough, we'll just go in a circle, won't we? Jane? Seriously, you look bad."

"I don't think we're supposed to walk around down here," Jane said.

"Sorry, I don't follow you…"

"Look." Jane stuck her hand through the shelf.

"Wow, brilliant!" Manali said. "How'd you know to do that?"

"I didn't. It was an accident."

Manali waved her fingers through the shelf. "Do you think we can climb through there, yeah?"

"I think so, but—wait."

Manali stopped. "What's wrong?"

"Gerhard said he heard a girl screaming inside the wall."

Manali pulled her hands back. "Where—here?"

"No, back there somewhere."

"So what do you think we should do?" Manali asked.

"I don't know."

"You're shaken up, yeah?"

"I guess so," Jane said. "I was wondering if maybe I should stop and let someone else do this."

"What?"

"I can't save anyone, Manali. I promise, I'm just an ordinary girl."

"We all are," Manali said. "Especially Thomas. All of us except you—Gaius said so."

"I'm serious. I don't want to do this."

"Why—because you're afraid you won't pass the tests or because you're afraid you *will?*"

"Both, I guess."

"Come on." Manali took her hand. "We'll crawl into the wall, and it'll be fine. Probably tons easier than walking on water, yeah?"

"A girl was screaming in—"

"—inside the wall, I know," Manali said. "If you keep arguing with me, there's going to be a girl screaming out here."

They both smiled, and Jane let Manali coax her to the shelf. Jane eased forward on her elbows and put a hand out in front; it vanished inside the back of the shelf. *She's right,* Jane thought. *This is the way I'm supposed to go. There's no reason to be scared.* She pulled her head closer, and more of her arm went in. *No reason to be scared. No reason. To be…*

CHAPTER 27

The Riddle

The room had the metal-salt smell of blood. It reminded Jane of the way her mouth tasted when she had a bloody nose. Manali helped Jane crawl out of the reverse side of the shelf. The room was squarish, with painted walls and a red-blue-green mosaic floor. The quiet, old pictures reminded her of a chapel. A little bearded man with goat's legs was slumped against the wall near a golden door. *What is that called?* Jane wondered. *A centaur? No, that's a half-man, half-horse.* Somehow Jane wasn't surprised to see him. But what had happened to him?

She walked across pictures of bobbins in armor and trees and the dazzling sun—all made from tiny, colored tiles—and the goat-man raised his hand to keep her away.

"Stop," he said. "Don't hurt me anymore."

"We aren't going to hurt you," Jane said, and she noticed a round hole—like a well—near the opposite wall. "Are you okay?"

"No," the goat-man said. "I asked him my riddle. *She* answered it, the little Egyptian girl. But he didn't. I've asked it so many times—each time Gaius needs to find another savior—and they all answer it. But he laughed at me. And he hurt me. He shouldn't have been able to do that. Someone must be helping him."

"Who hurt you?" Jane asked, but she already knew.

"The boy in the red coat."

Manali said, "Thomas."

"He came here before us?" Jane asked.

"Yes," the goat-man said. "He was just here."

"You said you asked him a riddle?"

"It's my job," he said. "I am the keeper of the second test."

"What's the riddle?"

"What do you leave behind as you make more?"

Manali shrugged. "That's easy," she said. "Footprints, right?"

The goat-man nodded. "It was harder five hundred years ago, when I invented it. The Egyptian girl answered it."

"Two kids came through here already?" Jane asked.

"Yes. But only one left."

Jane pointed to the hole in the floor. "What's that?"

"Go see for yourself."

As they went to the hole, Jane noticed the wall paintings. The colors were faded, like clothes that had been washed too many times, but there seemed to be a story. A girl met with a blind bobbin in a human city of airplanes and bombs. Next the girl walked over red water and then crept through a tunnel before standing in fire.

In the fifth frame, the bobbin—*Gaius,* Jane thought—gave the girl armor, and in the sixth frame, she fought a black shape that had been erased. The final, seventh picture was completely gone, as if it had been scrubbed off. *I wonder why.*

At the bottom of the hole—ten feet down—the African girl that had passed the first test lay dead on a giant pile of gold keys. Jane knew she was dead by the stillness—a strange stillness, as if she were a rock or a mound of dirt—and by the blood in her hair.

"Oh no!" Manali said. "We have to tell Gaius. She needs a doctor!"

There were ladder rungs on the side of the well—like those found in a sewer—and Jane climbed down. She pressed on the girl's neck the way people did on television when they were checking for a pulse. She didn't feel anything.

"I think she's dead," Jane said. The keys clinked when she sat back. "I'll call him. Gai—"

"No, Jane. You find the key," Manali said. "Whoever calls him is disqualified, yeah? Let me do it."

"Look at all of these keys," Jane said. "How am I supposed to know which one is right?"

"Try," Manali said, and before Jane could argue, she called, "*Gaius Saebius!*"

Manali was gone.

A moment later, the African girl's body had vanished too. *Thomas did that,* Jane thought. *He killed that girl. Why?* It didn't seem real. She examined the keys. There were thousands of them. She closed her eyes and concentrated, but nothing happened. They all looked the same.

This is pointless, Jane thought. She grabbed a key and climbed out.

"Tell Gaius to be careful," the goat-man said.

Jane paused at the golden door. *This isn't the right key,* she thought. *It can't be. I just picked it randomly.* "Careful of what?"

"If Castle Alsod is destroyed, the Raven King will win."

How could that happen? Jane thought. *No one can find the Castle.* But she said, "I'll tell him. After I try all these keys…"

The key fit. The lock clicked, and the door opened.

CHAPTER 28

The Chasm

Jane stepped into blackness—the kind of dark she only saw when she wore an eye mask late at night—and the door closed behind her. It was quiet. *Maybe all of those keys unlock the door,* she thought, *and the door is designed to open only three times. Or maybe I found the right key because I was meant to find it. No, that's silly.*

Gradually the blackness became gray in places as her eyes adjusted. *Somewhere in here is the third test.* The trial by fire, Gaius had called it. She stepped forward, reaching blindly. Another step and her shoe slipped off the edge of a drop—she lost her balance and fell backward, with one leg dangling over the edge. It didn't touch bottom. There was some kind of cliff in front of her.

Two girls are dead now because of Gaius and his stupid tests, she thought. It was strange to think about that. Jane had never known anyone who died before. *Except my grandmother,* she thought. *He killed her, just like he killed the bobbins. Just like he wants to kill everyone else. For no reason.*

She scooted back and stood again, searching for walls. There were none. She could see now that she was crouching on a semicircle of rock at the edge of a cave with a low ceiling and a long drop into blackness. Out there—ahead of her—was another rock platform just like this one, maybe forty feet away. *What am I supposed to do?* she thought. *Jump?*

Behind her, the door opened in a burst of light, and someone stepped in. The door banged shut again.

"H-hello…?" a boy said in the darkness.

"Gerhard?"

"Ah!" the German boy said, relieved. "Jane, are you here? I cannot see anything."

"Wait for your eyes to get used to the dark."

"Where are you?"

"I'm right in front of you, but don't move. There's a drop all around us."

"A drop?"

"We're on a platform at the wall of a cave."

Gerhard was breathing fast. "I think I see it now," he said. "What are we meant to do?"

"I don't know—maybe get to that platform somehow." She pointed across the chasm to the other one.

"How?"

"I have no idea."

Gerhard felt along the wall, and Jane said, "Be careful!" as he inched closer to the edge.

"Walk on water," Gerhard said. "The needle in the haystack— you left the key in the lock, so that was no problem for me—but this does not look like a fire trial."

"A trial by fire," Jane said.

"Yes."

"I know—maybe Gaius wasn't being literal. Maybe he just meant that the third test would be hard."

"This is impossible. No one can jump that far. And even if we can get over there, I can't see what's on the other side of that platform. It is too dark. We might be stuck out there, you know."

"I don't think we're supposed to jump," Jane said, and noticed the ceiling. Sure, it was uneven rock, but it wasn't far away—if she stretched, she could almost touch it—and there were handholds. Grooved, round handholds made out of rubber went in a straight line to the platform.

"Oh, no," Gerhard said.

"We're supposed to climb." *Hand over hand,* Jane thought. *I've never been good at that. My arms aren't strong enough, and this is way too far. He's right—it's impossible.*

Gerhard jumped to grab the first handhold. "Climb out there? This is a joke, do you think?"

"No, I don't think so."

Gerhard pulled himself up and dropped back to the platform. He laughed uneasily. "If I fall…"

"You're right," Jane said. "Let's look for another way."

"No. It's just—if I fall, tell them I made it to the third test."

CHAPTER 29

Handholds

"Be careful." Jane's palms were clammy, and her pulse was fast. "Wait, maybe you shouldn't—"

"It's easy." He grunted and pulled himself up, one arm, then the other. Gerhard paused, hanging over the pit. He was five feet away from Jane and thirty-five feet from the other side. He huffed again and grabbed another handhold—and again. Then he went slack. He was eight feet out.

"Jane?" Gerhard called.

"Yes?"

"I don't think this was a good idea. You know?"

"Come back!"

"I can't climb backward!"

He was right, she realized. The only way to return now would be to make it to the other side and turn around. Why hadn't she thought of it before?

"You can make it!" she called.

Gerhard grunted and kept moving. Left arm, right arm, over and over, and then he sagged again, his legs kicking, fists on the handholds. He was twelve feet away.

"How far down do you think it is?" he asked.

"Keep going!"

He did. Fifteen feet. Farther and farther. When he was halfway there, Gerhard stopped again.

"I can't," he said. "My arms are too sore!"

"You have to!" she shouted. "Go! You can do it!" There were tears in Jane's eyes. *I don't want to watch him fall,* she thought. *Can't I help him? Can't I do anything? Did Thomas make it across?* "Go, Gerhard!"

He continued over. Twenty-five feet away, almost thirty, and his right hand slipped. He shouted something in German and found his handhold. He was crying with exhaustion and terror and murmuring in German.

"Don't stop!" Jane yelled.

He pulled and groaned and fell slack again. Then again. Each time he grabbed a new handhold, his arms slumped from the strain. She could see his muscles trembling. He was five feet from the other side. *Don't fall,* she thought. *Please.* Another handhold. A pause. Another, and his fingers slid again—found the grip. He was almost there. Two more.

"I have to stop!" Gerhard called. "I have to—"

"No!"

"I can't—"

"*Go!*" Jane shouted.

He found another handhold and then, with his legs bicycling from the exertion, he had the last one and was across. Gerhard dropped onto his back on the second platform.

"You made it!" Jane said. "You're there!"

He crawled away from the edge and dragged himself up. "Thank you, Jane."

"What do you see?"

He walked in a slow circle around his platform. At last, he said, "Nothing."

CHAPTER 30

One Champion

Nothing?"

"I can see another wall and a platform with a door, but it is too far away, and there are no handholds." Gerhard slumped to the ground. "But even if there were," he said, "I can't climb anymore."

"There must be handholds," she said.

"Nope."

This doesn't make sense, Jane thought. *Why is that platform there? Is this a joke? A trial by fire without fire—just a long, long drop…*

Wait.

Jane dug the envelope out of her pocket. The writing glowed.

> *Three Spells Inside,*
> *One for Fire, One for Escape,*
> *And One to Make the Evil One Break.*

One for fire, Jane thought, and she took out the papers. There was shiny writing on one of them. Just two words: *Ignatio vate.* That sounded familiar for some reason. Jane put the two blank sheets and the envelope away again, and she raised the *Ignatio vate* paper.

Gerhard called, "Jane, what are you doing?"

She waited. Nothing happened. "Um…"

"What is that in your hand?"

Grandma Diana said these words, Jane thought. *She said them when she fought the Raven King in our living room.* "I'm not sure," she said. "It's a spell, I think. It says, *Ignatio vate—*"

Fire burst from the paper in tendrils that splashed along the walls and swirled like a river of fast-moving lava. The spell paper burned to ash, but the fire didn't go away.

She saw the path.

A narrow glass walkway extended from the left side of the platform, zigzagging along the walls, all the way to the opposite door. Even in the swirling heat and light, Jane couldn't see the bottom of the pit. It might go all the way to the center of the world and out the other side.

Curled in a fetal position, Gerhard yelled, "Jane, what are you doing?"

"It's okay," she said.

The fire streaked over their heads, rushing to flow along the walls. Jane followed the path—turning when it turned, slowing at the narrow curls, and hopping over two brief gaps—all the way to the opposite platform and door. The fire went out.

"J-Jane…?" Gerhard said.

"Yes, Gerhard?"

"Good luck saving the world."

"Thank you," she said and opened the door.

Inside, a golden hall led to steep stairs and a final door at the top with white light coming out of the edges, as if there were a huge lamp on the other side. Thomas was two steps from the door.

"There you are," he said.

Thomas was already there. *No!* Jane wanted to scream.

"You beat me," she said.

"This is funny," he said. "Only one of us is supposed to be here."

She reached the stairs and started up. "Why don't we work together?"

"Did you listen at all to what Gaius said? He only wants one savior."

The hall flickered black, as if Jane had blinked—but she hadn't blinked.

"We're both here," Jane said.

"I can see that. *I'm* not blind."

He killed that girl, Jane thought, only three steps below Thomas now. "What do you want to do?"

"What do *I* want?" Again the light sputtered, as if someone were playing with the blinds. But there were no windows. "What I want doesn't matter," Thomas said. "It's what *he* wants that's important."

"I think Gaius will—"

"Not Gaius, stupid. Gaius is a blind old cat with a farting dog that pretends to be a dragon. Gaius doesn't matter, and anyway, he'll be dead soon. I'm talking about *him.*"

Jane felt cold. "You've seen the Raven King?"

"Of course I have," Thomas said. "And you know what? He doesn't like you."

He kicked Jane hard in the chest, and she went tumbling and crashing and rolling down the stairs. Her left ankle twisted, and she banged her head at the bottom.

"Good-bye, Jane."

Oh, no!

Thomas went up the stairs to the door and went inside. *I've got to stop him,* she thought, *I have to—*

Before the door closed, Jane heard Gaius say, "We have our champion! Congratulations, Thomas!"

CHAPTER 31

The Race to Stop Him

The hall and stairs bled like a painting in the rain. The light and colors smeared and then reformed: Jane was back in her bed at Castle Alsod. Finn stuck his head in the door and said, "Welcome back, Jane! How did it go?"

"I'm okay." As Jane stood, pain flared in her left ankle. "Ow!"

"You don't look okay. Sit back down, and tell me what happened."

"No. We have to stop him. We have to warn Gaius. Help me to the door please."

Finn let her lean on him on the way out. "What happened?" he asked. "You didn't win…?"

"No. I was at the end—I almost…but he stopped me."

In the firefly-lit hall, Finn said, "Jane, I'm sure Gaius sent you back here to rest for a reason."

"I can't rest," she said. "Didn't you hear me? I have to stop him."

"Who?"

She steadied herself on Finn's side. *My ankle hurts too much when I walk,* she thought. *I have to catch my breath.* "Thomas."

"He passed the trials?"

"Yes," she said. "But I did too. So he kicked me down the stairs."

"What?"

"He knows the Raven King—I think Thomas is working for him."

Jane felt the muscles in Finn's shoulders tense, and he said, "Climb onto my back." She did, and Finn kicked open the door to the castle stairs. "Gaius and Thomas are at a ceremony with the animals—hold on…"

CHAPTER 32

The Soldier's Forum

They're at a place called the Soldier's Forum," Finn said. "It's not far."

They burst out of the swamp and were soaring low over a wheat field that rippled like the ocean in the wind. On a distant hillside, Jane saw a mass of animals. The animals covered the grass like giant ants, and above the hill, the sky was clouded with birds. Something was already happening.

"Is that it?" she asked.

"Yes," Finn said. He flapped his wings harder, and they jerked in quick spurts, like a car trying to switch to a higher gear. As they rushed nearer, Jane realized that it wasn't just one hill; three hills formed a valley, and all three were completely packed with elephants, horses, dogs—and every animal imaginable—all in a tremendous, orderly gathering. They were listening to someone.

When Finn flew over the heads of the animals at the back, Jane heard shouts of "Hey, no pushing to the front!" and "Don't block the view!" They cleared the summit of the hill. The valley below was even more jammed than the surrounding hills. And there, at the center of the valley, standing on the open grass, were Gaius, Thomas, and a flightless bird with an enormous head. The bird was maybe three feet tall, and as Finn dove closer, Jane realized that it was a dodo bird. *They're extinct, aren't they?* The dodo was offering Thomas a slender, armored chest plate that had been made to fit a girl like Jane.

Gaius's voice echoed through the valley, as if he were using a microphone (he wasn't) or the valley itself were designed to carry speeches (it was):

"...has saved the life of the champions who have come before you, this armor will also protect you, Thomas. It protected Diana Starlight..."

Thomas accepted the armor, and it grew and changed to fit his body.

"Stop!" Jane shouted.

Finn barreled closer and then swung into a spiraling dive. They landed at Gaius's feet. A group of hippos and nearby hyenas started muttering, and soon the entire valley was talking.

Jane jumped off. "He is working for the Raven King!"

Gaius said, "Jane—"

"Please, I'm not making this up! Don't—"

"Stop!" Gaius raised his stick. "What are you doing here, Jane? And you, Finn? I'm very disappointed."

"I had to warn you," Jane said. Thomas's face was bright red. Was that embarrassment or anger? she wondered. "Thomas cheated. He only won because he kicked me down the stairs."

Gaius asked, "Is that true, Thomas?"

Thomas said, "Of course not."

Gaius sighed. "You're lying. You *did* kick her. Why?"

Thank you! Jane thought. *Gaius gets it—he won't let Thomas hurt anyone else.*

Thomas seemed to shrink a little bit, and he stared at the ground as he said, "I'm sorry. You said only one of us could win."

"Did you tell Jane that you work for the Raven King?"

Thomas swallowed. "I'm sorry. I don't…"

"Did you?"

"Yes."

The animal chatter grew louder, and Gaius said, "Quiet, please." His voice carried; the talking stopped. "Why did you say that, Thomas?"

"I wanted to scare her," he said. "I shouldn't have done that."

"No, you shouldn't have. But you're right. Only one of you can win. And it is you, Thomas."

"But he kicked me!" Jane said.

"You're right, Jane. I don't approve of that," Gaius said. "But let me ask you this: If you won and then you found the Name of the World—as Thomas will do—what do you think the Raven King would do to stop you? Do you think he would kick you if he could?"

"What? I don't believe this! Thomas just said he works for the Raven—"

"No. He said that he told you that he works for the Raven King to scare you. My dear, there are good and evil, and there is also fate. Thomas comes from a great family, just like you. We all have a destiny, Jane. This is not yours." Thomas was still scowling at the ground, but she imagined that his eyes were laughing. "Take her back, Finn," Gaius said. "Tomorrow, you'll go home."

Jane squeezed her frustration and sadness into her fists. "What about all the other bobbins?" she said. "Was it their *destiny* to die? Was that *fate?*"

Gaius closed both hands on his cane. The dodo backed into the crowd, and the birds scattered overhead.

Behind her, Finn said, "Come on, Jane."

"Fine," Jane said. Thomas met her gaze as she walked away. He looked like he wanted to punch her. "I don't care," she said. "I'll leave."

Finn helped her onto his back, and they took off.

"At least you get to go home," Finn said, and Jane burst into tears.

CHAPTER 33

Breathe

Back at the castle, Jane and Manali ate dinner in silence. The mechanical crabs served steaming, homemade pizzas—some with extra gooey cheese, others with pepperoni and sausage, and still others stacked with pineapple and anchovies—but the dining hall was subdued. Children were leaving. Every few minutes, Gaius came in and called someone's name: "Erica?" or "Jason? It's time to go." The kids said good-bye quietly and then left. Animals escorted them through the swamp and back across the plains to the bobbin ruins and the elevator home.

It was over. They had arrived at Castle Alsod ready to make friends and pass the tests, and just like that, it was time to return to the real world. *Soon maybe we'll wonder whether this was even real,* Jane thought. *I'll never see Manali again. Somehow Thomas or Gaius—someone—will defeat the Raven King, and everything will go back to normal. I'll have to go to school again, and Mrs. Alterman will still be waiting for that overdue library book. I'll still have to take spelling tests and—*

"Jane?" Manali was watching her. "You should eat something, yeah?"

"I'm not hungry."

"It was a bad fight with Gaius?"

"Yes," Jane said. "In front of—everyone. Gaius picked Thomas. He didn't believe me...or he didn't care. Anyway, maybe he's right. Thomas *did* beat me. I wasn't strong enough."

"He *kicked* you," Manali said, then more quietly, "and he did the other thing too."

She means he killed that African girl, Jane thought.

Gaius came in and called, "Phillipe? It's time to go. Come with me, please."

A boy at the other end of the hall followed Gaius into the entry hall. Kids said good-bye, and when the door shut, the room was quiet again. Any one of them could be next. No more Hotland or dragons or Castle Alsod; time to go.

At the end of dinner, Finn called Manali, and she said to Jane, "Maybe I'll see you again, yeah? Stay yourself, Jane."

"Okay." Jane swallowed. "Bye."

Manali left.

Soon the dining hall was empty except for Jane and a scattering of other kids. Back in Jane's room, Finn said, "I can keep you company tonight if you want."

"Thank you," Jane said. "But do you know what the worst part is? I really thought I might be the one who's supposed to save everyone. Gaius almost had me convinced." She got into bed.

"It's no big deal," Finn said. "You'll see."

"You're right," Jane said, her stomach still jittery with emotion. "I guess I'm ready to go too."

Later, with Finn settled on the carpet, Jane stared at the gray ceiling and thought about Thomas, Gaius, Grandma Diana, the Name of the World. *I'm forgetting something important,* she thought. *Someone told me something…* She was getting sleepy—too sleepy to think anymore. *I'll remember in the morning,* Jane told herself. *Now, it's too late and…*

A shadow was growing on the wall, like an ink spot. Jane stared, suddenly wide awake. Her heart pounded as the shape stretched—it was coming through a crack in the stone—and she opened her mouth, but her tongue was too dry to speak. The shadow grew larger and became humanoid, with deep black holes—like skull sockets—in its head and giant, amorphous hands. It was a stickman, a sansi, like the things that had come after them at her house when the Raven King fought Grandma Diana and—

Wait. Stop, she told herself. *Slow down. Breathe.*

CHAPTER 34

The Attack

F inn! Finn, wake up!" Jane whispered, but the dragon didn't stir. "Finn!"

The sansi oozed across the wall, and now a second shadow started to squeeze through the crack. The first sansi reached for Jane. She jerked backward and fell off the bed onto Finn. Finn said, "Wh-what?" Then he saw the sansi and shouted, "Jane, come on! *Now!*" They scrambled out the door, and Finn said, "Get on my back!"

Finn ran down the steps, past one door, then stumbled to a halt: another sansi was rising—slowly, like a balloon—up toward them.

"Finn…!"

"Don't let go!" Finn shouted, and he kicked open the door with the hands painted on it.

Inside, a three-story library—with walkways and ladders around each level—led to a room with a massive table surrounded by silver suits of armor. Down a corridor of black torches, they stopped: a dead end. A stained glass window filled the wall with pictures of bobbin knights, dragons, and a girl with curly hair.

"Right," Finn said, turning about. "It's too bad my fire breath won't hurt these guys. I guess we have to go back…" Three sansi entered the corridor, blocking their path. "Or not. Ideas?"

The sansi moaned liked sick children.

"The window," Jane said. "Can we go through the window?"

But the last time, Gaius was waiting on the other side, she thought. *What if he's still asleep? He may not even know he's in danger.*

The sansi crept closer, their hands reaching.

Finn backed up. "Right," he said. "Cover your eyes, this may—"

The window exploded.

The blast of sharp glass knocked them onto the stone, closer to the sansi, and Jane shouted, "Finn, get up! We have to—oh, no!"

Thomas was outside the window, riding a leathery beast with the face of a diamondback snake and round insect wings. The winged snake flapped closer, and Thomas jumped inside through the broken window. There was fire behind him. Outside, the swamp was burning—flames crawled up the trees and spread across the water—and the sudden rush of smoke stung Jane's eyes. Thomas was wearing the armor—Grandma Diana's armor—that the dodo had given him.

Jane crawled backward. The sansi were close behind them, and now Finn groaned and tried to stand. His scales were streaked with blood and broken colored glass.

"Your dragon is hurt," Thomas said. "That's a shame. I'm going to kill him first…"

Jane raised her right hand and yelled, *"Ignatio vate!"*

When nothing happened, Thomas laughed. "I'm sorry, was that—"

She took out the envelope—*One for Escape*—and found a second paper with new writing on it: *Aven saat.*

"*Aven saat!*" she yelled.

"—supposed to hurt me or—?"

A bolt of lightning snapped from the paper into Thomas's chest plate in a white blast that kicked him into the wall. The second spell paper shriveled to dust in Jane's hand.

"Up!" Jane said to Finn. A sansi reached for her. "Come on!"

Finn staggered to his feet.

Thomas shook his head as if he'd been tackled and said, "How did you…?"

Jane jumped onto Finn's back, and as he ran to the window, she said, "You're not too hurt to fly, are you?"

Finn shouted, "We'll see!"

They cleared the jagged glass. When the flying snake hissed, Finn whipped it with his tail. The dragon beat his wings faster, and they were rising up, up—through the burning trees and over the swamp. Behind them, Castle Alsod was burning. The Purple Marsh—all of it—was on fire.

"We have to go back!" Jane said. "We have to help Gaius!"

"You can't do anything for him," Finn said. "We are lucky to be alive, and Gaius can protect himself."

"Where are we going?" Jane asked. The fires had faded behind them, and they were flying in complete darkness.

"To the bobbin ruins," Finn said. "It's the only safe place."

Jane said, "No, we have to—"

"*You can't,*" Finn said again. "Without the Name of the World, you can't stop them. If you go back now, you'll be killed. I'm sorry."

I can't just leave Gaius, Jane thought. But there was nothing she could do.

They flew all day and night, and when they reached the ruins—still full of animals—Jane thought about Grandma Diana's spells. *There's something else,* Jane thought. *Something I'm forgetting. Grandma Diana gave me…*She remembered the purple stone. *Grandma Diana told me to smash it or something,* Jane thought, *but I put it under my pillow. It's probably still there.*

"I have to go back to our house," Jane said. "On topside Earth, I mean." She told Finn about the stone and then said, "I have to find it."

As he landed at the elevator doors, Finn said, "Good luck."

"What?" she said. "You can't come with me?"

"I have to go back for Gaius now."

Jane said, "But I thought you told me that was pointless! How will you—?"

"I thought Gaius would meet us," Finn said. "But he isn't here. There's no time to argue! Go!"

When Jane started to protest, Finn took off, flying back the way they had just come.

I hope my family is okay, Jane thought as she got in the elevator. The stone might not be the Name of the World, but it was a place to start.

The elevator went dark, and when the lights came on, she was alone in a cramped, rickety elevator. It stopped at the top.

CHAPTER 35

The Return

Out of the elevator, Jane walked through blackness—her shoes loud on the stone floor—then abruptly stumbled into daylight. She was back in the park, and the sun was just coming up. The soft yellow light cast long shadows. She was almost home.

All that was *real,* Jane thought. But now, walking on the sidewalk past familiar suburban houses, she began to wonder. The porch lights were lit on every doorstep. *There's nothing odd about that,* she told herself. *It's early in the morning—no one's had a chance to switch them off yet.* In the early sunlight, Jane couldn't tell whether the lights were on inside the houses. *So what if they are?* she thought. *They're just lamps and light bulbs—nothing to be scared of.*

She walked in silence for a long time. This felt wrong. There were no birds. *They're in Hotland,* Jane thought. *I saw them.* But that wasn't what was bothering her. It was the lack of cars; the streets were empty. Sure, it was early, but *someone* should have been out, going to work or school or the grocery store. Where was everybody?

Several corners later, she spotted her house at the end of the block. It looked the same as it always did. The porch light was on, just like all the others.

She stopped at the edge of the front yard. The neighborhood was as quiet as if it had just snowed. But it was springtime.

Maybe I shouldn't be here, Jane thought. *Maybe the stone is just an ordinary marble. But what else can I do? I don't have food or money, and for all I know, it might be like this everywhere. The Raven King is doing this,* she thought. *He's distracting the adults with electricity and machines so they don't even notice that all the birds are gone.*

"This is not a good idea," she told herself softly.

Jane went up to the porch. The front door was open.

CHAPTER 36

The Trap

The television was still on, along with all the lights in the front hall and the lamps—everything was the same...except that Jane heard only a metallic drone from the TV and static on the radio upstairs. She looked into the living room. The television screen displayed colored, vertical lines. The remote control was missing, so she turned it off manually.

"Hello?" she called. "Mom? Dad? Michael?"

Something rustled, and Jane spun: Michael was cowering behind a chair in the corner.

"They won't look at me," Michael said. "Jane, Mom and Dad won't..."

She ran to him and took his hand. Michael was trembling. "Stay with me," she said. "Come on."

With Michael behind her, Jane went to the hall. She was about to turn for her bedroom when she saw something in the kitchen out of the corner of her eye. A thin, gray-eyed man sat at the table, cradling a cell phone in both hands. His chin stubble and the dark lines around his eyes made him look lost and old. A fragile woman sat beside him, so pale and motionless that she might have been made out of cardboard.

"Dad?" Jane called. "Mom?"

Her parents didn't stir. Michael squeezed Jane's arm harder as they approached the kitchen.

"Mom? Dad?" she said again. "Are you all right?"

Her father squinted at the phone as if he thought her voice might be coming from it. As they entered the kitchen, Jane could see that her dad's lips were cracked and chapped. Her mother's eyes were half-closed, as if she'd been drugged. *Haven't they eaten?* Jane thought. *Haven't they had a drink of water in all this time?*

Jane went to the cabinet and found two glasses. Her hands wouldn't stop shaking. She turned on the sink faucet. Nothing happened. She jiggled the handle and tried again. No water came out.

"I'm sorry," Michael said. "I was scared. I didn't know…"

"It's okay," Jane said. "Dad? When was the last time you had something to drink?"

When their father didn't answer, Michael said, "We have to get out of here."

Jane tried the refrigerator. There was leftover broccoli casserole, burritos, ketchup, and milk. She grabbed an orange juice carton and poured two glasses, then returned to the table and placed the glasses in front of her parents. They didn't move.

As Jane got the casserole out of the fridge, a big cockroach crawled across the kitchen table. She stared at the roach. It was fat with long antennae.

Still her parents didn't move.

Michael said, "I don't know what's wrong with them." He

jumped away from the sink. There were centipedes, roaches, pill bugs, and silverfish crawling out of the pipe.

"I shouldn't have come back," Jane said, but her legs were shaking. She smelled something sweet and sick, as if the casserole were covered with mold. But it wasn't rotten.

All the lights went out—even the daylight. A man in a torn, bloody cape was standing in the room. It was as if he'd been there all along, and now that the light had changed, she could see him. Jane tasted acid-fear. *We have to run,* she thought. *Why won't my legs move?* She heard something beating, like drums or wings. She dropped the casserole dish and heard it smash on the floor.

"Hello, Jane," the Raven King said.

CHAPTER 37

Run

"Where is it?" The Raven King's voice was calm, and a moment after he spoke, Jane couldn't remember the sound. She couldn't see his face—only the outline of his body and dark cape.

"I don't know," she said.

"I *will* hurt you if I have to, Jane. But first I will hurt your mother, father, and brother. Do you understand me? Think for a moment before you answer," the Raven King said.

Michael said, "Leave us alone!"

The Raven King was closer. One moment, he stood near the wall; the next, he was behind her parents, an arm's length from Michael and Jane.

"I'm sorry," she said, reaching into her pocket. "I don't know where it is. I can't give it to you." She took out the envelope and fumbled open the last paper.

Three Spells Inside,
One for Fire, One for Escape,
And One to Make the Evil One Break.

The last page said: *Bas ravel.*

"What is that?" the Raven King demanded.

Jane raised the paper and shouted, *"Bas ravel!"*

The paper brightened, as if it were a dirty window someone had wiped clean. On the paper, Jane saw a mountain made out of shiny black rock, dark clouds, and a brown sky. The paper was showing her a mountain in Hotland. Now the picture faded, and the paper and envelope crumbled like old leaves. The pieces fell away. *A mountain,* Jane thought. *How does that help me?*

The Raven King said, "I will ask once more, child. Where is—?"

Jane and Michael ran into her bedroom, and when Michael opened the window, it smashed back down, just missing his fingers. The Raven King stood in the doorway. Jane knelt beside her bed, but before she could reach under the pillow, a desk lamp jumped and hit the side of her head.

Jane was shaking. "I don't know where it is!"

"You're lying!" the Raven King said. "What did you see?"

"Please," she said. *Don't cry,* she told herself. Jane felt helpless, like a cornered animal. She was breathing hard. "I don't know!"

The room flickered like a scratched record, and Jane saw the shadow of a bird with a hooked, bloody beak. "Do not"—a bolt of black like the opposite of a flashlight beam shot at Michael, and he slumped to the floor—"lie to me."

Jane lunged at her bed. There was Grandma Diana's marble, right where she left it. She threw the marble at the wall, and it shattered like glass. The window flew open in a whirlwind of papers and books. A golden shape rushed through the window and hit the Raven King like a wrecking ball. He didn't fall, but he was in the hall now, as if someone had shoved him out.

A woman's voice said, "Be still, children." Soft arms scooped up Jane and Michael and carried them through the open window and into the sky.

Panting, Jane watched the houses and treetops grow smaller until she could see blocky neighborhoods passing under her dangling feet. She craned her head. A woman with golden skin and a white cape carried them. They were flying. This was impossible. The woman was beautiful—not like a person but like a mountain or a river or the sun. Jane heard the regular thump of wings, like a heartbeat, and although it was only a woman carrying them, when she closed her eyes, Jane saw a golden eagle.

CHAPTER 38

Rachel

Jane slept.

She woke to cold wind that burned her cheeks and tossed her hair. She was laying on a dark platform of tar, boxy air conditioning vents, and colossal antennae that looked like giant, blinking stalagmites—each as tall as an office building. Michael was asleep nearby. The golden woman stood at the edge of the platform, facing away, her cape fluttering in the wind. There were soft clouds around and above them. *But where are we?* Jane wondered.

As she approached the golden woman, something dropped in the pit of Jane's stomach, as if she'd swallowed a rock. They were on the roof of an office building—no, not just any office building. Below, the ground was a grid of skyscrapers and roads, and there was water, like the ocean or a big lake, not far away. They were so high that she could see past the downtown buildings to miniature neighborhoods leading all the way to the horizon; they were so high that there were clouds below them—and smoke. Tiny puffs of soot-colored smoke rose here and there.

Although Jane had never thought of herself as being afraid of heights, just watching the golden woman standing on the ledge of the building—what seemed to be *miles* above the ground—made Jane's legs wobble.

"Where are we?" Jane's voice was swallowed by the wind.

"A safe place obviously," the golden woman answered without turning. "I can hear anyone coming for miles."

"But what are all those buildings down there?"

"Chicago."

Chicago, Jane thought. *This is the Willis Tower, the tallest building in America.*

"Are there fires down there?" Jane asked. "Is something burning?"

"Yes."

"Please don't stand on the ledge," Jane said.

The golden woman stepped away and said, "Call me Rachel."

"Thank you for saving us."

"You called me with the Wishing Stone, you know. Are you Diana Starlight's daughter? You seem very young."

"She was...she *is* my grandmother. You called that purple marble a Wishing Stone...?"

"It was the last bead from Justinia Lovelock's necklace."

Jane said, "Justinia who?"

Rachel sighed as if Jane were back in class, wasting time with easy questions. "A long time ago, I gave a girl a necklace with special beads so she could call for my help. Justinia was the first person to save us from the Dark One."

"She was the first person to stop the Raven King? And you're a Great Eagle, one of the twelve eagles that..." Jane tried to remember what Finn had told her "...that protected people and everything, right? So you're *not* dead?"

"Not yet, no," Rachel said.

"Are the other eagles still alive?"

"That's complicated. I haven't seen them in a long, long time—how's that for an explanation?" Rachel crouched beside Michael. "Your brother is dying, you know." Rachel lifted his shirt. There was a dark smear like a shadow growing in the center of his chest.

Jane's heart was racing. "What is that?"

"The Dark One struck him. The poison will spread, and when it covers Michael, your brother will become a shadow like the others."

A sansi, Jane thought. *Michael will turn into one of them.* "What can we do?"

Rachel said, "The only way to stop the poison is to stop *him*."

"And I need the Name of the World to do that," Jane said. "What is it?" When Rachel didn't answer, Jane said, "You won't tell me? Then why are you here? What's the point if you won't help me?"

"You misunderstand, little girl. I'm not here to guide you or counsel you—think of me as a weapon to protect you. I *will* help you, but I can't lead you," Rachel said. "The Wishing Stone means that I will grant your wishes, but I can't tell you what to do. That's up to you, not me."

"Like a genie or something?" Jane said. "Then I wish to have the Name of the World and kill the Raven King."

"It doesn't work like that, Jane. I'm strong, not all-powerful."

"Is everyone frozen like my parents? How much longer can they live like that?"

"Not long," Rachel said. "Civilization is forgetting itself. But clearly not everyone is standing still—hence the smoke. Soon everything is going to get much worse. In another day, maybe two or three, the Dark One will win. You are part of a very small group that was not seduced by technology."

I won't panic, Jane thought. *I need to think about what I have to do—there isn't much time.* "So you can't tell me anything," she said. "But you can help me. Okay, my grandmother was the last person to use the Name of the World, right? When was that?"

"In 1945."

Grandma Diana was my age back then, Jane thought. "Can we go to London?" she asked Rachel. "How long will that take?"

"Yes, of course we can. As I fly, it will take several hours," Rachel said.

But I can't waste several hours, Jane thought. *Michael is dying, everyone is in danger, and for all I know, the Raven King could be waiting for me at Grandma Diana's apartment now. I wish Thomas was* the champion, *and I didn't have to do this. What if the Name of the World isn't at Grandma Diana's apartment anymore? And if she did still have the Name of the World there, why didn't she bring it with her to America when she came to visit? She didn't know the Raven King would show up, that's why.*

What if I'm wrong?

"We have to go," Jane said. "I guess I don't have a choice." And in her best Grandma Diana voice, she said, "Take us across the pond, dear."

CHAPTER 39

The Burning Island

Before reaching the Atlantic Ocean, they stopped in New York City to get food. Jane had never been to Manhattan before, but she had seen it enough times on television and in movies that she expected to see a massive metropolis. It should have looked like a grid of office buildings with a square slice of trees, Central Park, at the center. Now the city was buried under brown smoke that made Jane's eyes water. She tasted hot cinders that burned the back of her throat.

As they dropped lower, the soupy air cleared, and Rachel brought them down on the sidewalk of a wide avenue of glass buildings with banks, clothing stores, and all-night convenience shops on their bottom floors. Everywhere there was broken glass, and bodies cluttered the sidewalk, as if there had been a stampede or a riot. The streets were jammed with yellow taxicabs, blue sedans, buses, and cars—all motionless and empty. Some of the cars were just burnt-out shells. Black smoke rose from sewer grates and open manholes. Fires raged inside nearby buildings. Jane heard a man screaming in the distance and a random popping sound, like firecrackers. The traffic lights at a nearby intersection changed from red to green; the red *Don't Walk* hand turned into a white *Walk* person.

"Be quick," Rachel said. "I'll watch from that rooftop. Call my name when you're ready." She flew onto the roof of an office tower.

Michael said, "It looks like a war." He pointed past the carnage. "Is that Times Square?"

A few blocks away, Jane saw the flashing lights and restaurants of Times Square, just like on television on New Year's Eve. The intersections were crowded with crashed cars, and she saw more bodies. Jane spotted people walking through the square with long sticks—spears or rifles, maybe—in their hands.

"Yes," Jane said. "I'll be right back. Do you want roasted peanuts for the flight?"

Michael was already asleep again. His poison wound made him groggy and confused. When Jane checked under his shirt, the blackness had almost spread to the top of Michael's stomach.

In a nearby convenience store, a balding man slouched behind the counter. His shirt was covered in blood. A woman was waiting to pay for sandwiches and soft drinks, which she'd placed on the checkout counter. She was staring at the static on a television above the door and holding a tiny pistol in her left hand. In her right hand, she held a dark blue smartphone just like the one Jane's mother used to have.

The woman didn't look down. *It's all right,* Jane told herself as she stepped quietly past the woman to the refrigerators to get sodas and prepackaged sandwiches. There were bloody smears on one of the refrigerator doors. *The only way I can help them is to stop the Raven King,* Jane thought. When she had filled a paper bag with food, she turned for the exit. The woman was staring at her.

"Why won't he call me back?" the woman said. She shook the

phone. "I can't check my email." She started to cry and tapped the gun against the side of her head.

Jane's pulse was loud in her ears. "I'll fix it," she said. "Please, don't do that."

"I just want to hurt someone," the woman said, and she cocked the gun.

"Rachel!"

The woman aimed the gun at Jane.

Jane shouted, "Wait—!"

The pistol clicked. It was empty.

Rachel was standing in the doorway behind the woman. "We have to go," she said. "Right now."

"That woman…"

Rachel grabbed Jane and picked up Michael, and they took off in a sharp rush of air that almost made Jane drop her bag of food. Below, the smoke thinned, and they flew fast over more houses and towers on their way to the ocean.

Rachel said, "You're safe. Be quiet and try to rest."

But Jane kept looking at the empty sky behind them. Soon they were rushing over water with sailboats and barges lolling on the low waves. The water darkened, the air got colder, and the land faded behind them. Jane drifted to sleep.

She dreamt of fire.

When she woke, Jane was hanging in Rachel's arms, her sack of deli food clenched in one hand. They were still over the ocean, but there was land on the horizon.

Rachel said, "Jane? You were screaming."

"I'm fine," Jane said. "Is that England?"

"Almost," Rachel said. "That's Ireland. We'll be there soon."

"How is Michael?"

"Worse."

What if I'm wrong? Jane thought. *What if the Name of the World isn't here and I brought us all the way across the ocean for nothing?*

"I can beat the Raven King, right?" Jane said. "If I find the Name of the World, I can do it, can't I?"

"You have to try," Rachel said. "Sometimes you must fight even when you know you can't win. Do you understand?"

"Yes," Jane said, but she thought to herself, *I'd call that answer a big no.*

CHAPTER 40

The Triangle

London was the same as New York.

Jane had hoped that here—all the way on the other side of the ocean—things might be different. But as they approached the towers and sprawl of London's suburbs and followed a train line—past train cars that were stopped in a neighborhood of red warehouses—into the center of the city, Jane saw black clouds. Below the smoke, the streets were burning and full of bodies; every car was stopped. London was old, with low buildings in a disorganized scramble of parks, statues, museums, churches, and stores, but Jane knew where she was going. They had visited Grandma Diana here two years ago. On that trip, Grandma Diana had explained in great detail how to find her apartment. *Flat*, Jane reminded herself. Grandma always called it a *flat*, not an apartment.

"That dome is Saint Paul's Cathedral, Jane," Grandma Diana had said. "Do you see it there? Good, now watch how those buildings—that white one and that ugly green tower—form a triangle with my flat at the third point. Do you see it, Jane? That's how you'll remember where I live. The triangle."

Now that she thought about it, Jane wondered if Grandma Diana had somehow known that this would happen and that someday Jane would have to return to London on her own. The directions made the most sense looking down from the sky. *No,* Jane thought. *How could Grandma Diana have known this would happen? And if she did know, why didn't she warn me?* Then Jane realized, *She did warn me. She gave me the Wishing Stone, and she sent me a letter with three spells. And now all three spells are gone, and I'm on my own.*

Jane instructed Rachel to follow the massive dome of Saint Paul's Cathedral north, using the white and green buildings as guideposts to find Grandma's apartment. Soon they landed on cobblestones in front of 45 Dialer Street. It was a simple, tree-lined block, and here too, the buildings' windows were cracked or smashed out and spewing filthy smoke. Jane heard people shouting, and far away, she heard sirens. Wind thrashed the tree branches. There were buzzers under the intercom with a list of the last names of the people who lived in the apartments, but when Jane tried the buzzers, nothing happened. The door was heavy and locked.

"I didn't think about this," Jane said. "We don't have a key, and no one is going to answer. What are we supposed to do now?"

Rachel touched the doorknob. It turned by itself, and the door opened. "It's just a door, Jane," she said. "I've handled much tougher situations."

Grandma Diana lived in 3G on the ground floor. They walked through a lobby of flowery wallpaper and found Grandma Diana's door at the end of a dark hall.

"Can you do that again?" Jane asked, and Rachel opened the door. "Thanks." But they didn't go inside.

If this is a trap, Jane thought, *now would be the time for the Raven*

King to appear. The apartment hall looked just like Jane remembered it: The left wall was lined with overflowing bookshelves; photographs—including two of Jane—hung on the right wall. The hall led to a parlor with old couches covered in plastic, and Jane knew that the door on the left went into a small kitchen. The doorway on the right would take them to a living room and then another hall with two bedrooms and a bathroom.

They waited in silence until finally Jane stepped in. *Rachel is right behind me,* she thought. *If anything happens, she'll protect me.* Michael blinked awake in Rachel's arms.

"Where are we?" he asked.

"Grandma's apartment," Jane said.

"What's wrong?"

A floorboard creaked around the left corner in the kitchen. They stopped.

"It's all right," Rachel said.

Jane looked in. Grandma Diana's tortoise cat, Sammy, was perched over a gigantic, open bag of cat food. Sammy meowed and rubbed against Jane's leg. The faucet was dripping. They walked through the apartment slowly. Jane examined ceramic lamps, a wooden mask hanging on the bathroom wall, expensive dishes, photographs, and paintings, and she finally said, "This is hopeless."

CHAPTER 41

Grandma Diana's Flat

Grandma Diana used her second bedroom as an office with a desk heaped with papers, folders, and notebooks. The office walls were a chaotic jumble of bookshelves. Nothing was neatly stacked; most of the books were piled on top of things, ready to fall at any minute. Beside a fern under the street-side window, there were locked filing cabinets and a wastebasket full of crumpled tissue, wadded papers, and empty fountain pens. Grandma Diana had been a teacher and then a librarian before she retired, and Jane's mother usually referred to her as a writer, although as far as Jane knew, her grandmother had never written a book. Now Jane wasn't so sure. There might be a book—there might be *seventeen* books—buried in this office.

The Name of the World is probably in here, Jane thought. *But there are so many interesting little things*—a Dutch model ship, a ring with a yellow skull on it, finger bones in a glass case—*and any one of them could be the Name of the World. How am I supposed to know?*

Grandma Diana's bedroom was less intimidating. There was a small, carefully made bed, a cross on the wall, more framed photographs, and folded clothes. Unfortunately some of the office clutter seemed to have jumped across the hall carpet: books, cassette tapes, pens, and notepads covered both bedside tables and the blue chair in the corner. No wonder the Raven King had hounded Grandma Diana for the location of the Name of the World. Hunting for it in this apartment would be like looking for a needle…

Jane sat on a couch in the parlor. The plastic crinkled and stuck to her legs. Sammy jumped onto her lap and purred.

"I need your help," Jane told Rachel. "Please."

"Sorry, Jane," Rachel said. "Even if I could tell you, I don't know where the Name of the World is now. I *can* tell you that you're running out of time."

"Thanks."

Grandma Diana grew up in this flat as an only child, Jane thought. *What was it like back then? After she beat the Raven King, where would she hide the Name afterward? Under a floorboard or in a crack in the wall? This is impossible.*

Back in the office, Jane picked through the pages on the desk, careful to remember where everything went so she could put it back. Why? Grandma Diana wasn't coming home. Rachel watched from the doorway, still holding Michael.

"It's not here," Jane said at last. "Or if it is, I don't know where…I give up." She kicked the desk and slumped into the chair. It was the only clear place in the room. "I can't believe we came all the way here for nothing."

Michael pointed to a picture hanging behind Jane. "Who is that?"

Jane turned in the swivel chair. It was a black-and-white photograph of a dark-skinned man in a suit seated under a big umbrella at a table in a garden. A young woman in a stiff Victorian dress sat across from him, squinting in the sunlight, a teacup and saucer in her hands. The outdoor table was set with blurry tea shapes. A servant stood in the background, and behind him, Jane saw thin trees and a wall. *Huh.* On the table, beside the teapot and a black knife that looked like a fancy letter opener, there was a handheld mirror. In the photograph, the mirror was dark and ornate. The longer Jane stared at it, the more out of place the mirror seemed, as if it had fallen out of the sky. It didn't fit.

In the bottom right-hand corner, someone had scrawled *'03, In Deepest Need* and an illegible name that started with *T*. Below those words in newer ink, someone had written a long string of numbers. *Like a code,* Jane thought.

"Why did you notice that picture?" Jane asked Michael.

"I don't know," he said. "My chest started to hurt when I looked at it."

"What do these numbers mean?" Jane asked, and she read them aloud. There were fourteen digits. "*In deepest need.* That's not Grandma Diana in the picture. That must be her mother—or maybe even her grandmother."

"Our family has been doing this for a long time?" Michael said. "Maybe it's a message, like coordinates or something..." He winced. "This really hurts. I have to leave this room please..."

As Rachel carried him back into the parlor, Jane frowned at the numbers. *This is it,* she thought. *This is something important—maybe the combination to a safe...?* She checked behind the picture: nothing. *I am close. What can you use numbers for? Birthdays, ATM codes...*

She moved the papers off one end of the desk and lifted the receiver of an antique rotary dial phone. There was no sound.

"Rachel...?" Jane called.

Rachel came back and touched the phone. When Jane raised the receiver again, there was a dial tone. Jane pulled the circular dial all the way around with each number, and when she finished, the line was quiet. It clicked. And then it rang. Jane's heart caught in her chest. It rang again.

A girl answered. "Hello?"

"Hello, I'm sorry to call like this," Jane said. "But I found this number, and if anyone there knows my grandmother or maybe someone knew my great-great grandmother—I'm trying to find an old black hand mirror..." Silence. "Hello?"

The girl on the other end cleared her throat and said, "Jane...?"

Jane's hand tightened on the phone. "Hi, Manali."

CHAPTER 42

Two Families

Jane, how did you get my telephone number? Where are you—you're still in America, yeah? Or are you *here*? Have you seen what's happening? It's crazy, like anarchy, yeah? Me and my cousins are here eating noodles, but the television and the radio—nothing works, you know? I didn't think this phone worked." Manali was talking fast, as if she'd been underwater and was releasing a mouthful of words as she came up for air. "Gosh, it's good to hear from you. You said you're here in Mumbai?"

"No, I'm not in India," Jane said. "I'm in London."

"What are you doing there? People are running wild in the streets, and nobody has eaten for days—the Raven King is doing this, yeah? I wish Thomas would hurry up and stop him. Are you okay? What's wrong?"

"Manali, I'm at my grandmother's apartment. Remember I told you she stopped the Raven King a long time ago? There's a picture on her wall with a woman and an Indian man having tea. There's a mirror on the table in that picture. I think that mirror is the Name of the World."

"I don't understand. I thought Gaius sent Thomas to deal with *him*."

Jane told Manali what had happened. Manali said, "Wow. But

how could a mirror be a weapon? And this is my uncle's phone I'm talking on now—how did you know to call this number?"

"The number is written on my grandmother's photograph."

"Really? How is that possible?"

"I think maybe our families helped each other a long time ago," Jane said. "Does this make any sense to you?"

"I don't know," Manali said. "What's the guy in the photo look like?"

Jane went for a closer look. "He has short hair, a beard, very dark eyes…"

Manali laughed. "That could be any man in my family, Jane!"

"In the photograph, they're in a garden. The man isn't smiling, but he's not as serious as most of the people you see in old pictures." Jane rubbed a smudge from the picture frame. "Well…"

"What? Is something wrong?"

"The man doesn't have a left arm." Manali was silent, and Jane said, "You can see by the way he's sitting—when you look closely—the sleeve is just hanging there. I think he's only got one arm. Manali…?"

"Yeah."

"Did you hear me? I said I think he's missing his left—"

"Yeah, I heard. My mother used to tell me stories—that's my great-great-*great*-grandfather, Turim."

Jane felt a rush. "That makes sense," she said. "There's a smeared signature at the bottom that starts with a *T*."

"But Turim wouldn't have had this phone number. Back then they probably didn't even have phones."

"The phone number is written in different ink," Jane said. "Maybe it was added later. What do you know about Turim? That may be my great—several *greats*—grandmother sitting with him in the picture."

"He lost his arm in a war, I think." Manali murmured to herself in another language. "You're sure about the picture, yeah?"

"I'm looking at it right now. Do you know of *anything* that might connect us? Have you seen an old mirror?"

Manali was quiet. Jane heard rustling, and then Manali said, "I'm back. I think I found it."

"The mirror?"

"No, a picture of Turim in our family album. Here's one that has a British woman standing with him." A pause. "And that's it."

"There's only one picture?"

"Only one," Manali said. "There are words at the bottom, but I can't read them. Looks like they're dated *'04*. Maybe 1904? Oh, wait, here's another one—not of him, but the British woman is in it again…and so are you."

CHAPTER 43

Bombs and Birds

Jane felt dizzy. "What?"

"It looks just like you," Manali said. "Like an older version of you anyways. There's one woman—the lady from the Turim picture, except she is much older in this picture—and there's a girl who looks like you standing with a couple of Indian kids and their parents. I haven't seen these pictures in years. All the people are standing on a dock with ships behind them."

"Is there a date?"

Manali hesitated. "Um…'46, I think, maybe '45—it's hard to tell. It's definitely forty-something."

"Does it say anything else?"

"Yeah, it says, *Protect and Keep Us from Bombs (1940) and Birds (1945)*."

"Is that it?"

"That's it," Manali said. "This phone call is going to cost you a fortune, yeah?"

Jane smiled. "It's worth it."

"I'm sorry I'm not more help. Funny that your grandmother had this number, isn't it?"

"It is…" Jane was thinking. "Wait just a second." She covered the receiver and asked Rachel, "The Germans bombed London a long time ago, didn't they? When was that?"

"Are you talking about the London Blitz?"

"What year did that happen?"

"That was 1940."

Bombs (1940).

Jane's pulse quickened and she said, "Thank you so much, Manali! I have to go." And to Rachel, "Where's the bomb shelter?"

CHAPTER 44

The Shelter

They found a locked door in the lobby (Rachel opened it) that led to steep wooden steps and a cement basement with brick walls. It smelled of mildew. A bicycle was chained to the bottom step, and the left wall and area behind the stairs were crowded with boxes with names written on the sides, along with words like *kitchen* and *breakables*. A coin-operated washing machine and a dryer were against the right wall under a paper taped to the bricks with detailed instructions like *Please DO NOT remove someone else's clothing*, *Wait your turn*, and *Management is not responsible for missing items*.

Jane was disappointed. "This is just a basement."

Rachel carried Michael down the steps. "It was used as a bomb shelter once."

"How do you know?"

"I was here when people hid from the explosions."

"Why won't you tell me more?" Jane said. "Why was my friend Manali's phone number—*in India*—written on an old picture in the office up there?"

"Obviously your families helped each other a long time ago—through several generations."

Why did I think Grandma Diana would hide the mirror in a bomb shelter? Jane asked herself. *Just because Grandma Diana came down here once doesn't prove anything, and besides, she hid here in 1940—five years before she beat the Raven King.* There were uneven gaps in the brick wall where pipes snaked out. Gaius had said to stay away from pipes. *I should search Grandma Diana's office again,* Jane thought. *I should go through everything—the mirror is probably up there.*

Michael screamed as Rachel carried him closer to Jane. "Stop—stop!" he shouted. "That hurts!" And when Rachel stepped back, he relaxed again, half-asleep.

Jane said, "Step forward again."

Rachel did, and Michael jerked up, yelling, "Ow! My chest! Stop!"

"Step back."

When Rachel moved away, Michael slumped and was quiet.

His wound reacted to the photograph upstairs, Jane thought, *as if the mirror in that picture—as if the Name of the World—were reaching out to burn him.* She stepped where Rachel had been standing when Michael screamed. She didn't feel anything, and the floor was solid cement. *What if it's buried under here?* she thought. *I would need someone to jackhammer it open or something. But what if it isn't...?*

She crouched at the nearest wall. The uneven bricks looked like crooked teeth, ready to fall out. She grabbed one and pulled. It didn't budge. So they weren't loose; they just looked like they were. She tried another one—nothing. And another. She tested the bricks as high as she could reach and then started pulling on them in the next column all the way down again. *It's probably under the floor,* she thought. *This isn't—*

A brick came out.

CHAPTER 45

Hidden Treasure

The loose brick was as high as Jane's waist. Carefully she placed it on the floor and reached into the dark gap. It was like a cubby inside the wall—the perfect place to hide a mirror.

"Ow!" Jane pulled her hand back out. She had pricked her thumb on something sharp. Blood pooled around the cut. "Can you use your powers or whatever to tell me what's in there?" Jane asked, and when Rachel shook her head, Jane thought, *Of course not.*

Slowly Jane reached in again. She felt hard, folded paper. Jane took it out; there were three sheets of unlined yellow paper with blue cursive writing on them. It was the same handwriting from the envelope and three spells. But it wasn't the paper that had cut her. She reached in again. Her arm tense, she poked and checked and finally touched smooth metal. Tapping it carefully as if it were a hot burner, Jane traced the side of the metal object to a soft handle. A knife. She grabbed the handle and pulled it out.

It was a narrow black knife, about eight inches long. Drawings that were as tiny as Jane's fingernails cluttered the blade—all the way to the mean-looking point. The first picture was a series of horizontal lines; then there was a dot with five lines sprouting from it; then a circle; then a jumble of vertical lines; and, finally, an upside down *V*.

Jane checked the hole again. It was empty. She showed the knife to Rachel. "Do you know what this is?"

"You can see for yourself."

Michael groaned and pawed his chest when Jane brought the knife closer, so she backed off to examine the old papers. They were tearing along the creases where they'd been folded. The first page read:

> *I destroyed the Dark One today with the help of Gaius Saebius and Tanya. I am writing this letter to you, somewhere in the future, whoever you are, so that you will know what I have sacrificed and why. He came to take revenge on the world by spreading madness. He thought that if people killed each other like animals, they would grow too wild and disorganized to resist him or to even notice what he planned. And he was right. No one noticed until it was too late. The adults were consumed by war. And the Dark One almost won.*

As Jane flipped to the second page, Rachel said, "Jane, someone is coming."

"Just a minute…"

> *But I found the Name of the World, and I learned the spells of fire, lightning, and sight. The hardest part was losing my brother, Sam.*

Jane paused. Grandma Diana was an only child; she didn't have a brother.

I sacrificed him so that the world could live. If I had to do it again, I don't know what I would do. I only know that inside the Steel Mountain, I made a choice. I let the Dark One erase my brother, my best friend—who I loved more than anything in the world—so that I could get close enough to stop him. He killed Sam—no, I killed Sam so completely that he has never even been born. I'm the only one who knows what I've lost.

"Jane…"

"Wait," Jane said. She remembered the mountain that the third spell had shown her. *Was that the Steel Mountain?* Jane wondered. *Is that where I have to go?*

"We may be in danger," Rachel said. "It's time to go."

Jane started reading the third page as she followed Rachel up the stairs.

Only the Name of the World could hurt the Dark One, but the Name is just a tool, like a gun. Without bullets, a gun is useless. Without sacrifice, the Name is useless. But I have stopped him now, so no one will ever have to fight him again. The Sharp Map guided me to the place where the Dark One first fell. That's where I traded my brother's life for the life of the world. God forgive me.

Diana Starlight, August 6, 1945

At the top of the stairs, Rachel stopped Jane with one arm. "Too late," she said. "Someone is here."

Jane stuffed the papers into her pocket and held the knife in one hand. It was heavier than it looked, like a paperweight.

"Who is it?" Jane said. "Sansi?"

"I'm not sure," Rachel said. "I hear someone from Hotland, and he is…"

Nails clicked through the lobby, and a German shepherd limped around the corner.

Jane ran to him. "Finn!" Finn wagged his tail. He was carrying a scrap of paper in his mouth, and one of his hind legs was bandaged. "Are you hurt? What's this?"

Finn dropped the slobbery note into her hand. Three words were scrawled in brownish red: *Gaius is gone.*

CHAPTER 46

No Choice

Outside, Rachel walked them to an old church on the street corner. "You can open the door to Hotland in many places, Jane," Rachel said. "But you know that if you go back to Hotland, I can't come with you."

As Finn whimpered and Rachel waited, Jane scanned the last page of Grandma Diana's old note again.

The Sharp Map guided me to the place where the Dark One first fell...

Jane held up the knife again. "Rachel, is it possible that this isn't *just* a knife? These lines—could they be some kind of map?"

Rachel hesitated. "It's possible."

"Can you take care of Michael while I'm gone?"

Rachel nodded. "I'll protect him as long as I can."

Jane kissed Michael's forehead, but he didn't even wake up. He was running out of time: the poison had reached the bottom of his neck.

"Okay, Finn, let's go," Jane said.

Rachel said, "Jane, the Dark One is much more powerful than he was the last time you visited Hotland. If you go back, you may not be able to return. Are you ready?"

"I might be stuck there? But I don't even have the Name of the World yet. I can't fight the Raven King without it, can I? I don't have any more spells—I'm not the savior. Gaius said so. Don't look at me like that, Finn. Rachel, tell him—explain that I'm not ready, like my grandmother was."

Rachel said, "Your grandmother was frightened too."

Jane felt very small. Learning that Grandma Diana had been scared made it even worse. "Then why did she do it?" Jane asked.

"She didn't have a choice."

"But how am I supposed to fight *him?* Is this a map of Earth or Hotland? It's just a bunch of lines and circles…" But that last drawing, the upside-down *V* could represent a mountain. *The Steel Mountain could be the mountain I saw in the third spell,* Jane thought. *But what if the Name of the World isn't there and the Raven King is waiting for me?* Jane said, "I'm not strong enough to beat him, am I?"

"No, you're not," Rachel said. "But you don't have a choice. Touch the church stones and ask them to open."

Jane did, and a low black doorway formed. She said, "Take care of Michael."

"Your brother will be safe here."

"Thank you," Jane said. "All right—come on, Finn. Let's do this before I change my mind."

Jane stepped into the wall.

CHAPTER 47

Claws

When the rickety elevator expanded, Finn became a dragon again, and he said, "I don't know where they took Gaius. When I went back to Castle Alsod, he was gone." The gymnasium elevator lights came on. One of Finn's gigantic hind legs was swaddled in bandages. "We need your help, Jane. We're in a lot of trouble here."

When the elevator doors opened, she saw why. The animals were gone. The old bobbin ruins were empty, and the grass was dead. The ground was so dry that it was cracked like a desert or a dusty eggshell. The daylight was faded and sepia-gray. A skin of ugly clouds covered the sky, and three points curled around the Hotland sun, as if a giant bird claw were squeezing it.

"What is *that?*" Jane asked.

"A spell," Finn said. "The Raven King's magic has spread everywhere."

"Where are all the animals?"

"Gone. The Raven King trapped them here and turned them into sansi."

Stickmen, Jane thought. *Like what's happening to Michael.* She showed Finn the knife: horizontal lines; the dot with five lines; a circle; vertical lines; and the upside-down *V.* "Do you see these pictures? I think it might be a map to someplace called the Steel Mountain. Do you know how to get there?"

"Yes, it's on the eastern side of the Old Wall," Finn said. "It's where the Raven King lives."

"The Raven King can't *see* the Name of the World," Jane said. "It's invisible to him. I think the Name of the World is on the Steel Mountain."

"You mean it's been sitting under his bed or something this whole time? I don't know—this is dangerous, Jane. Are you sure it's there?"

"No."

"Ooo-kay." Finn said. "Then what are we waiting for?"

Behind them, the elevator dinged. Manali stepped out. "You were just going to leave without me, yeah?"

"Manali!" Jane ran to hug her. "How did you get here?"

"I opened a door to Hotland in a phone booth three blocks from my house. Hi, Finn. Have you found the Name of the World yet? No? When this is all over, we'll get our picture taken to confuse our grandchildren. How's that?" After she climbed onto Finn's back, Manali said, "Hold on a minute. Where's Gaius?"

CHAPTER 48

How the Story Ends

I can't believe how quiet it is," Manali said.

After they left the bobbin ruins, they followed the Sunburn Road toward the Purple Marsh. They were still too far away to see much, but Jane could already tell that the marsh was gone. The horizon was swollen and black, like burnt plastic. *Everything is going to be like this if we don't stop him,* Jane thought. *The Raven King is like someone throwing a temper tantrum, breaking everything around him. I'm not afraid of him,* she told herself. But the nervous jags in her chest meant that wasn't true.

"If our grandparents could stop him," Manali said, "we can too."

Jane said, "I know."

"You're worrying too much, Jane. Your grandmother said a Sharp Map guided her. You've got the map—all we have to do is follow it to the Name of the World and the Raven King. Don't you know how stories like this end? The bad guy always loses."

"What if this is different?"

"Different how?"

"Different like Shakespeare," Jane said. "What if everyone dies at the end?"

"This isn't make-believe," Manali said. "We get to choose what happens."

They ate cold cucumber and lamb sandwiches Manali had

packed, and soon they reached the edge of the Purple Marsh. The trees were crumpled and black with ash, as if someone had emptied a giant fireplace over them. The red water had all dried up, and the air smelled like burnt popcorn. Nothing moved.

"Hellooo!" a voice called below.

Finn called, "Who's there?"

"Finn, you big dog, where have you been?" The lady frog—the same frog who had worn lipstick and let them enter the swamp with Gaius the last time—crawled out of a hole. "Do you see what he did to my swamp?"

"I know, Sandra. I'm sorry," Finn said. "I'm glad you're still here. You're the first one we've seen."

"The others are hiding," she said. "But there aren't many. Where's Gaius? I thought he'd be with you."

"No," Finn said. "They got him."

Sandra croaked in soft shudders, like a child trying not to cry. "The Raven King finally got Gaius too, huh?"

"Don't worry. We'll find him."

"Excuse me," Jane said. "Ms. Frog—"

"Just Sandra, dear."

Jane drew the black knife. "Have you ever heard of the Steel Mountain?"

Sandra disappeared into the hole. "Are you mad? Put that away, child! Away—away!"

Jane slipped the knife back into her pocket. "I'm sorry, I didn't know—"

"All of you, get! You'll have the sansi swarming like buzzards!" she shouted from inside the hole. "Go! Less talking, more flying, you big dumb dog!"

CHAPTER 49

The Crater

Big dumb dog," Finn muttered when they were airborne. "Sandra is lucky there's nothing left to burn down."

Jane said, "Finn!"

"What? Do I look like a dog to you? I'm a dragon. *Dra-gon*."

Manali said, "I don't understand why she would be afraid of the knife. Maybe she knows something we don't."

Finn snorted. "She knows diddly."

"Finn, if Gaius trusted her, I'm sure—" Jane's voice caught in her throat. "Is that...?"

"I'm afraid so," Finn said.

Ahead Castle Alsod was a crater. The great tree had been gashed right down the middle and torn open like a burrito that had burst in the microwave. The outer walls had been ripped apart, and hunks of marble, glass, smashed gears, and chair legs were scattered everywhere. Finn didn't land.

"Is she dead?" Jane asked.

"No," Finn said. "She's just badly hurt. But if Gaius doesn't come back to heal Alsod, she will die, yes."

They flew in silence until the ruined castle and swamp were behind them. The hills of the Soldier's Forum—where the dodo gave Thomas Grandma Diana's armor—were bare, and in the distance, a white wall crossed the plain. There were regular lines along its side, like the layers of a canyon. The wall was taller than the buildings in New York and it went on forever in both directions.

Finn said, "The Old Wall is the only thing still standing in Hotland that was here before the Raven King. Nobody knows who built it or why."

Jane looked at her knife again. The first picture was a series of horizontal lines. *And there it is,* she thought. *The Old Wall. We're almost there.*

CHAPTER 50

The Old Wall

The top of the Old Wall was as wide as a big river. On the western side, behind them, the daylight was hazy, and the ground was dust and weeds for miles. The eastern side of the Old Wall was different. Ahead the sky was black. Far below, the ground *squirmed*, as if it were covered with tin-colored earthworms. Lightning snarled through the blackness, and Jane glimpsed something—a giant tree?—standing on the distant plain. There was no thunder.

Jane's palms were sweaty, and every time the unnatural lightning flashed, she heard her heartbeat in both ears.

"Are you scared?" Manali asked quietly.

Jane's fingers were trembling, so she clasped her hands together. "No."

"I am."

I don't want to do this, Jane thought. *I just want to go back home and live a normal life. I don't even care if kids make fun of me at school or if Mrs. Alterman is angry because I didn't get my spelling test signed. I just want this all to be a dream. I want to wake up.*

"Are you ready?" Finn said.

Lightning flashed again, like a white-hot sword in ink.

Manali squeezed her hand, and Jane said, "Yes, let's go."

They flew into the darkness. The air was hot and thick, like dirty soup. Lightning flashed overhead, and Finn flew lower so Jane had a better view of the ground. At first she thought it was covered with snakes or worms…but it wasn't. They were pipes. The ground was a nest of iron pipes with gaping ends that looked like suckers or mouths. Jane shivered.

Lightning struck the ground with an electric charge that made Jane jump. All the hair on her head and along the backs of her arms frizzed and stood up. Finn flew faster and closer to the ground. Jane heard the pipes creaking and whining, like the joints of a mechanical animal. The pipes were reaching up. *It's my imagination,* she thought. But it wasn't; the pipes were trying to reach Finn.

In another lightning flash, she saw that the tree shape ahead was actually a colossal hand blocking their path. As big as a mountain, the rust-iron hand was frozen as if someone—*something*—had been buried while he was reaching for the sky. *We're too close!* Jane thought. *If we don't go up, we'll crash into the wrist!*

Finn pulled up, beating his wings so hard that Manali slid backward and Jane screamed, "Finn!" They raced higher, rushing over the palm of the hand, toward a gap between the thumb and forefinger.

"Almost there!" Finn shouted. "Don't let—"

Lightning struck his wing.

CHAPTER 51

The Tolec Hand

Like a bug hit by a flyswatter, Finn dropped.

Manali yelled, "Jane!" and rolled off. They weren't high above the hand's palm—maybe ten feet—but they were moving fast, and as Jane fell with Finn, the metal hit her shoulder hard. She cartwheeled and bounced—and stopped.

Jane's right leg was dangling off the edge of the palm, one hundred feet above the swarm of pipes.

"Jane, are you okay?"

Jane rolled away from the edge, and Manali helped her up. Jane was bruised and her elbow throbbed, but nothing seemed broken. She could walk. Finn was worse. He slumped against the hand's thumb, his right wing shredded and smoking. He groaned as he sat up.

"Is everyone all right?" he called. "Everyone but me, I mean…?"

"We're okay," Jane said. "Are you hurt?"

"Of course I'm hurt. I got struck by lightning." Finn smiled and twisted his broken wing onto his back. "We were lucky. If that had hit us over the pipes, we'd be worm food by now."

"What are they?" Jane asked.

"The pipes? On topside Earth, pipes swallow just about anything you put in them—water, food, you name it. This is where all those pipes come out. But these pipes haven't eaten anything in a long time, so they're hungry."

"Lucky we landed up here," Manali said.

"Lucky for now," Finn said. "This is the Tolec Hand. A long time ago, the Tolec Giants tried to take over Hotland. The Raven King didn't let them."

Lightning flashed, and in the light, Jane saw that the blanket of pipes ended at a curl of pale ground ahead. *It's so close,* she thought. But it was still too far away to jump or glide to—and they were too high anyway.

"The thing is," Finn said, "the giants were made out of metal. Do you know what happens when electricity touches metal?"

"Metal conducts electricity," Jane said.

"Exactly. Which means the next time lightning strikes this hand, we'll all be fried to a crisp."

Manali said, "Are you sure you can't fly? Can we jump or glide or something?"

Finn checked the distance across the last pipes. "No. It's too far." Lightning zapped a nearby pipe in a burst of sparks that shook the hand. "But I guess we have to try. Get on my back—quickly!"

Manali climbed up, but Jane didn't move.

"Did you feel that?" she said.

"Jane, get on," Manali said.

"Are the Tolec Giants dead?" Jane asked. "Is this hand connected to a body underground?"

"I have no idea," Finn said. "Now hop on."

"Listen, I don't think we can jump that far. You hurt your wing."

Finn said, "We don't have a choice."

"Tickle him," Jane said. "Blow fire on his fingertips."

"Are you joking?"

"It's too far," Jane said. Lightning snapped and just barely missed the pinky finger. The hand shook again. "See?" Jane said. "Come on, Finn. Tickle his fingers!"

When Finn started to protest, Manali said, "Jane's right, Finn. Give it a try."

Finn took a deep breath that puffed out his chest like a bird and then leaned forward, as if he were sneezing in slow motion. Fire shot out of his mouth like water from a garden hose. The flames sprayed over the tip of the thumb, curling in waves around the enormous fingernail. The hand shuddered; the fingers flexed down.

Lightning flashed behind them. *We're almost out of time,* Jane thought. *Move, you stupid giant! Move!* Slowly the forefinger curled down, down—until the tip touched the giant palm at the base of the thumb...

Manali shouted, "Jane!" and Jane scrambled onto Finn's back as the gigantic forefinger flicked them off. Finn grunted as the fingertip walloped his butt, and they were thrown like a piece of fluff. Finn flapped his good wing, and they spun in a crazy loop as lightning flashed on both sides. The pipes rushed closer, closer— and Finn made it over, crash-landing on the smooth rock.

CHAPTER 52

The Stone Lake

Finn was upside down, but the pale ground reflected his right-side up reflection. "Nice idea," he grunted.

"We're alive, aren't we?" Jane said. Something about the reflection bothered her.

Manali brushed herself off. "Well done, Jane. Seriously, we never would have made that jump."

Finn rolled over. Behind them, the Tolec Hand lit up as lightning struck it.

"Manali is right," he said. "A-plus, Jane."

Ahead the pale ground went on and on as far as they could see. It was reflective like glass but murky like frozen milk, and it was completely flat. The sky was still black, but the lightning was behind them now.

Jane checked the knife. The horizontal lines represented the Old Wall; the dot with five lines was the Tolec Hand. Next came a circle. Just a circle.

"This is the Stone Lake," Finn said. "I think we should be able to walk straight across."

"I can't see the other side," Manali said. "Are you sure?"

Jane said, "It's a circle on the Sharp Map…"

"Hop on," Finn said. "Let's keep moving."

As they started across the Stone Lake, Jane watched their

reflections. What kind of rock could make a reflection like that? She realized what was bothering her about it: The stone only reflected them. The stone surface should have been black from reflecting the sky—but instead it was white.

"I don't like this," Jane said. "Why is it called the Stone Lake? Doesn't a lake have water?"

"How should I know?" Finn said.

Jane stiffened. "I was just asking."

"I only know it's called the Stone Lake," Finn said. "That's it."

"Fine," Manali said. "Geez."

The way Manali said that irritated Jane, as if Manali thought both of them were stupid.

"You know, you can go back if you're still scared," Jane said.

Manali smirked. "Why? Because you don't need me all of a sudden? You're the savior who is going to fix everything all by yourself? You sure needed me a little while ago, when you called me in Mumbai. At Castle Alsod, I only let you sit with me because I felt sorry for you—not because I like you."

"You're right," Jane said. "I *don't* need you. You're not the one who has to fight the Raven King. You're just going to stand back and watch."

Finn shook, like a wet dog, and they went tumbling off his back. "I can't stand listening to you two," he said. "Find your own way across." He turned back. "I'm not a baby-sitter."

"No, you're a big dumb dog," Manali said, "and you can't even fly straight."

"And you're a brat," Finn said—and then to Jane, "But Manali isn't as bad as *you*. We're all going to die here because of you."

"I didn't ask you to come along," Jane said. "You came to me, remember? Do you think I want to do this?"

"Then why are you here?" Finn said. "You don't have any more spells, and the Name of the World might not even be at the Steel Mountain. The Raven King is probably just sitting there waiting for us. Did you think of that?"

"Of course she did," Manali said. "She's thought of everything, yeah? She's the *savior*."

"And you're just the stuck-up sidekick," Jane said. "You just came along to watch me die, *yeah*?"

Manali reddened. "Shut up, Jane."

Jane raised her fist. "*Shut up, Jane.*"

Manali said, "Put your stupid hand down."

Finn huffed flames. "Maybe I should just drop-kick both of you back to those hungry-hungry pipes. Like this…"

Jane noticed something, and she shouted, "*Wait!*"

They stopped. Jane looked back at their reflections. In the reflected stone, Jane and Manali were still riding on Finn's back, casually talking. When Jane saw the image on the Stone Lake, her mind cleared like someone with blurry vision putting on glasses.

Jane murmured, "What are we doing?"

Manali laughed. "I'm going to break your nose."

Jane pointed at the ground. "Look."

Now Finn saw it too. He said, "Don't argue please. Climb on."
They did.

"Keep watching it," Finn said. "Don't look away from the stone.
You have to do what your reflection does or you'll stop being you.
The Stone Lake will twist your personality…"

So Jane watched, and when the reflection-Jane raised her hand
to brush back her hair, Jane raised her hand to brush back her
hair. When Jane's reflection spoke silently to Manali, Jane apolo-
gized, and Manali—still watching her own reflection—said, "I'm
sorry too."

"Me three," Finn said, imitating his reflection. "And I can
already see the other side. We're across!"

As the girls rode Finn off the pale stone, a chill passed across the
back of Jane's neck. *There is it,* she thought. *The vertical lines…*

CHAPTER 53

The Forgotten Woods

A skeletal forest grew at the bottom of a jagged black mountain. It was the same mountain Jane had seen in the third spell paper. To get there, they would have to go through this forest. There was no dirt; the trees grew right out of the iron-slab ground like street poles. The forest was leafless and gray, and when a cold wind rushed down from the top of the mountain, the trees rattled *crisp-crisp*, moaning like a thousand sad voices.

Manali said, "Finn, are you absolutely certain you can't fly?"

"I wish I could," he said.

Manali looked at Jane. "I'm sorry—I *am* scared. I don't want to go through this forest."

"I didn't mean what I said before," Jane said. "But I don't think there's another way up. The Sharp Map shows these up-and-down lines. I think they're supposed to be trees."

Manali stared at the gray forest. "They don't look like trees—they look like bones."

Finn said, "Jane's right. There's no way around if we want to go up the Steel Mountain."

Jane approached the edge of the forest. "Does this place have a name, Finn?"

"I think it's called the Forgotten Woods. It has some

connection to someone in your family. Not to Diana Starlight—to someone long before your grandmother." He frowned. "I can't remember."

"Whoever made this knife went through this forest," Jane said. "That means we can make it too."

The wind howled again. The trees swayed with a noise that sounded like crying, and Jane heard the word, "Mary..."

"Right-o," Finn said to Jane. "You go first."

As Jane stepped between the first trees, the air got colder. Manali and Finn were right behind her. *Mary,* Jane thought. *Who is she, and why does that name sound familiar?* The forest constricted, as if the trees were creeping closer. *But that's silly,* Jane told herself. *Trees can't move.* Then she remembered the grove of apple trees back at the bobbin ruins—the place she'd hidden from the kangaroo. Those trees had thrown apples. There Jane had uncovered an old statue of a girl wearing an armored chest plate and ancient clothing, holding an apple and...a black knife. The Sharp Map. *The girl in that statue was called Applepatch Mary,* Jane thought. *And* Traitor *had been carved over the statue's plaque...*

Jane said, "Finn, who was Applepatch Mary?"

The wind shook, and the overhead branches scraped like claws. The forest moaned, "Go away!"

"She's the one connected to this forest," Finn said. "But I can't remember what she did. Anyway, there are no apples here."

The wind cried, "She betrayed us!"

Manali said, "Did you hear that? It sounds like the wind is talking."

The trees were close now, and Jane ducked under a low branch.

"Maybe there *is* another way around," Finn said. "I don't think the trees want us here."

"I don't understand," Jane said as she walked deeper. "Why would the trees be angry?"

The wind howled. A branch smacked the back of Finn's head, and as he yelped, a second branch snared his tail. A third branch pinned his front legs. "Hey!" he shouted. "Let go!"

"We are not trees!" the wind screamed.

Manali said, "Finn's right—this forest is crazy! We should go back!"

But Jane stood her ground. "Of course you're trees…"

As the trees pushed Finn to the ground, he said, "I'll burn you all down if you don't let go!"

A branch snapped around his snout, like a muzzle. "Stop it!" Jane said, and she drew the black knife.

A low branch pulled Manali into the air—"Jane!"—and the trees leaned closer to Jane. Finn thrashed, but each time he was about to break free, more branches latched onto him. A tree limb cracked open, and a white mist, like powder or pollen, coated Finn's head. He closed his eyes and fell limp, like a sack of potatoes.

"Let him go!" Jane said. A branch snagged her shirtsleeve, and she twisted away. "I'm warning you!"

The wind moaned, "Forbidden! Traitor!"

Overhead, Manali shouted, "Run, Jane!"

No, Jane thought. *I will not run from these trees! This is the only way through. It's on the Sharp Map.*

Another limb split open above Manali, and white dust sprinkled her face. She slumped and stopped struggling.

A tree limb coiled like a thick rope around Jane's wrist. When she tried to hack at it with the knife, another branch slapped her arm down. Roots swallowed Jane's feet. Now a branch hugged her waist, and she couldn't move her arms. She was trapped.

The trees shook. "We are cursed." Branches were squeezing Jane's chest too tightly. "We do not want to grow."

She tried to move her left hand and the knife, but her wrist was twisted down; if she struggled, the blade would stab her own arm, not the branches.

"We want justice, not peace."

"Please," Jane gasped. "Stop!"

"Sleep," the wind murmured. A branch snapped over Jane's face, and the powder—it smelled like sap and flowers—covered her face. She held her breath. "And never wake up."

At last she couldn't help it. Jane gasped for air. She breathed deep, swallowing the powder, and the forest was—

CHAPTER 54

Pancake Time

Jane? Jane, it's time to wake up."

"Huh?" Jane sat up in bed. Early morning sunlight filled her bedroom. Her father was smiling in the doorway dressed in his navy blue robe and pink bunny slippers.

"You sounded like you were having some serious dreams," he said.

Jane didn't know what to say. Her bedroom looked just like it always did. There was the usual mess of books, papers, and clothes. And there was Iz, safe and sound in his glass iguana tank.

"Is everything okay?" her father asked.

She wiped sleep from her eyes and put her bare feet on the carpet. It felt real. A moment ago she had been in a talking forest with a dragon and a girl from India…A dream. All of it was a dream. Of course it was.

"Everything is fine," Jane said.

"Good," her father said. "Mom is making pancakes. They should be ready in a few."

After he left, she heard him knock on Michael's door to wake him up. Jane's pulse was still racing, and she could almost feel the trees grabbing her arms. She rubbed her wrists, clapped her hands, and smiled. There was no Raven King or Hotland. It was all imaginary. But it had felt so real.

She went to the bathroom and then looked in Michael's room. He was already at his computer, checking his email.

"Good morning," Jane said.

"Hi," he said. "The pancakes smell good." He was right; they did. "Is breakfast ready yet?"

"I don't know," Jane said. "Michael, did anything happen last night?"

He frowned. "Like what?"

"After I went to bed, I thought—I guess I dreamed—that all kinds of things happened. Really weird things."

Michael shrugged and kept clicking his mouse. "They were just dreams," he said.

"Is Grandma Diana still here?"

"I think so. She got stuck in the storm and couldn't go back to her hotel, remember? I'm just glad the power is back on."

Their mother called from the kitchen, "Breakfast!"

Michael hopped up, and they both went in to set the table. Already seated, Grandma Diana was drinking a cup of tea beside their father. He was flipping through the newspaper.

"Good morning," Grandma Diana said. "I trust we slept well."

Michael set the plates and glasses while Jane arranged the forks, knives, and spoons. *Everything is back to normal,* Jane thought. *I'm so happy it wasn't...why are there butterflies in my stomach?*

When they were all eating, Jane's mother said, "Jane, is something wrong? I hope the storm didn't keep you up."

Before Jane could answer, Michael said, "Mom, after breakfast, can I listen to the iPod again?"

"We have a few errands to run today," their mother said. "And Grandma Diana was talking about a trip to the park."

"Do we *have* to go to the park?" Michael asked.

Grandma Diana smiled. "We don't *have* to do *anything*, Michael. I thought it might be pleasant. I understand they have playground equipment."

"That's only for little kids," Michael said.

"I'm sorry," Jane said, swallowing. "I have the strangest feeling right now…"

Her father touched her forehead. "Are you all right?" he said. "You look pale, Jane."

Jane coughed. Each time she breathed, her chest stuttered like a balloon that wouldn't fill all the way. "Grandma Diana, the stone you gave me yesterday…" Jane wheezed. "In my dream last night, I used it to—"

Her father grabbed her hand. "Jane! I don't like the way she looks."

"I'm sorry, dear," Grandma Diana said. "I'm not sure what you're talking about. I don't recall giving you a stone."

"A Wishing Stone," Jane said, and she staggered into the hall. "I put it…" Her vision filled with spots.

Behind her, Jane's father said, "Call an ambulance! Jane, sit down!"

"Under my…" Jane stumbled into her bedroom and collapsed at her bedside. She couldn't hold her eyes open. She couldn't catch her breath. Jane fumbled under her pillow. There was nothing there. It wasn't real.

It was, Jane thought. *I know it was.*

Somewhere far away, Jane's father was shouting, "—to the hospital right now!"

Her mother was speaking on the phone, "…I don't know—oh, God, she just fell…"

Wake up, Jane told herself. She slumped forward and tried to breathe, but no air came. *Wake up. Applepatch Mary has something to do with the trees that don't think they are trees. What did Finn say back at the apple grove? Applepatch Mary tried to save the bobbins, but she couldn't. I knew Gaius was hiding something—the bobbins didn't die. The trees…*

Jane dropped to the floor. *Wake.* She imagined her hand moving the black knife. *Up.*

CHAPTER 55

Mary's Bargain

Pain flared in Jane's left wrist, and she cried out, sucking air, like a fish on the beach. She was back in the forest; she had stabbed herself with the knife. The trees were still squeezing her, waiting for her to stop breathing.

"You should not be awake," the wind moaned.

"And you shouldn't be trees," Jane whispered. "You're bobbins."

The branches let go, and Jane fell hard. She could breathe again. Coughing, she begged the bobbin-trees to release Manali and Finn. They did.

"The Raven King turned you into trees," Jane said, "didn't he?"

"Yes."

"But Applepatch Mary—" Jane tried to think as Finn and Manali regained consciousness. The Raven King didn't *kill* the bobbins; he transformed them into hollow trees. And they were angry. "Mary couldn't break the curse. You wanted her to change you back into bobbins, but she couldn't do it. So she—" *What?* Jane thought. *Get it right or this forest will crush us again.* "Mary tried to help you live like trees. She taught you how to grow fruit, didn't she?"

"*Make peace,* Mary said. *Accept that you are cursed.*" The wind rose, and the entire forest screamed, "But we are warriors and defenders of Hotland!"

"You are all bobbins," Jane said. "If you let us go, I'll fix this. I'll make the Raven King change you back."

Finn murmured, "The only way to do that would be to defeat him…"

"Do you swear it?"

"I'll do it," Jane said. "Please…"

The trees relaxed, and the branches moaned: "Mary saved this world, but she was a traitor to the bobbins. Do not betray us, Clear Eye."

Clear Eye? Jane thought, and she said, "I won't. I promise."

They walked in silence until the trees ended on a steep slope of sharp rock at the base of the Steel Mountain.

"That was brilliant," Manali said. "Thank you, Jane."

I'm so tired, Jane thought. She stared up at the mountain. *I have to stop and rest just for a minute.* The Steel Mountain was the last marking on the Sharp Map. *This is where Grandma Diana said the Raven King first fell into Hotland, and according to her letter, this is where she fought him. I saw this on the third spell paper.* But the Steel Mountain was enormous, and the climb was straight up sheets of razor-sharp rock.

"Now what?" Finn said.

Jane found a handhold. The rock cut into her fingers. "Now we climb."

CHAPTER 56

The Steel Mountain

They climbed until Jane's arms throbbed, and Manali begged her to take a break. But she didn't let them stop. *There isn't time,* Jane thought. When a slab of gray rock broke away under Finn, he threw himself at the side of the mountain, dragging all four sets of claws in the stone. The broken slab dropped, dropped, and smashed in half far below.

Jane pulled herself higher, searched for another handhold. The rock cut a line of blood in her palm as she climbed up. Her muscles were trembling with the exertion. Cold sweat stung her eyes as she continued up.

"I can't…" Manali said below her. "Please, I have to stop…"

Jane closed her eyes and pulled with both arms—and as her fingers slipped, she caught herself—but her arms wouldn't work, and she sank back to her first perch. She tried again, crying out as she lost her handhold once more.

"Be careful!" Manali said. "Jane!"

"We have to keep going," Jane said. Her hands were slick with blood and iron grime. "We have to…" She stared up at the mountain. It went on forever.

Finn crawled up alongside Jane and then he rolled, huffing, onto a cliff above Jane's head.

I can't do this, Jane thought. *I'm sorry. I'm not as strong as Grandma Diana was—Manali's right; I'm too tired.*

A claw grabbed Jane's wrist, and before she could yelp, Finn pulled her onto the cliff beside him. There was a cave in the side of the mountain.

This is it, Jane thought. *We're here!*

Finn helped Manali up, and they stepped into a vast cavern with walls that shimmered with flakes of red. The room was narrow and tall, and it ended at an empty black throne with red wings painted on the wall behind it—as if the chair were ready to fly away. The cave smelled like coal and ash. There was no way out.

A dead end, Jane thought. *This isn't it, after all.* Wait—there! She ran to the back wall: The mirror was embedded in the rock, like a fly frozen in amber. It was as if the translucent stone had somehow formed around it.

"There it is," Jane said. "Finn, can you help me get it out? We have to break open the wall!" She found a heavy rock and smashed it against the stone. The rock cracked. "Manali, get another rock and—"

"Jane…"

Jane turned. "What?"

Thomas stood in the cavern entrance, smiling.

CHAPTER 57

Dark Magic

As Thomas approached, he said, "Is that it? Is that the Name of the World inside that wall?"

Jane hammered with her rock again. A hunk of stone fell away, exposing the mirror's handle. She grabbed the handle and pulled. The mirror budged, but it didn't come out.

Thomas was still wearing Grandma Diana's armor. "I appreciate this," he said. "You led me straight to it. The Raven King can't see the Name of the World, but *I* can."

"Stay back!" Manali shouted. "Don't—"

Thomas raised one hand and said, "*Nova shun!*" A bolt of red light knocked Manali into the wall. She collapsed.

"It'll take more than a flashlight to handle me, boy," Finn said. "You're about to tango with a dragon."

"Really?" Thomas pointed at the ceiling. He called, "*Nova shun!*" again, and the red light ripped stalactites away in an avalanche that buried Finn.

Jane pulled harder on the mirror's handle. Still it wouldn't break free. *Come on!*

"The Raven King's magic is much more powerful than Gaius's little spells," Thomas said. "I can use this spell over and over and over again. But you're all out of spells, aren't you? That's too bad."

Jane braced all of her weight on the handle, but it was no use.

Thomas raised his hand. "*Nova shun!*"

Pain exploded in Jane's eyes, and she fell against the wall. Her chest felt like it was on fire.

"I'll tell you what I'm going to do," Thomas said. He picked up a rock and began to chisel out the Name of the World from inside the wall. "First, I'm going to take this mirror out. And then, I'm going to kill you and your friends."

Jane tasted blood.

"There." The mirror broke free. Thomas frowned as he examined it. "*This* is what all the fuss was about? I've got to be honest, I'm a little disappointed. After all of that, I figured it would be something more dramatic, you know?" He raised his foot at Jane's face. "You know what? I've wanted to kick in your head since the day we met."

Thomas brought down his heel, and Jane grabbed his ankle and twisted hard. He fell with a startled shout. The Name of the World clattered to the ground.

"You stupid…" Thomas raised his hand. "*Nova—*"

Jane grabbed the Name of the World.

"*—shun!*"

The red light bounced off the mirror and hit Thomas's face. He shouted and flopped backward.

Slowly Jane stood, wincing at the pain in her chest. *I have it!* she thought. *Now where is—?*

The throne wasn't empty after all.

CHAPTER 58

The Confrontation

The Raven King watched with his hands folded. Jane couldn't see his face, but a hooked beak curled out where his mouth and nose should have been. A small gray tree grew on his left side, and the mannequin of Grandma Diana—with blue marble eyes and a frozen face—was propped on his right side. Sansi covered the walls of the cavern; they blocked the exit. They moaned like a dying ocean.

"Put that down," the Raven King said. He sounded bored. Jane felt younger as she approached. *The Raven King is so old and cruel,* she thought, *and who am I? I'm a little girl—that's all.*

"You," Jane said. She tried to sound brave. "You have to…let us go and—"

"Put it down," the Raven King said. "I will not ask again."

"I'm not afraid of you anymore."

The Raven King was suddenly standing. "Yes, you are." There were black wings on his back. Jane heard distant bells, like a funeral at a cathedral. There were bugs crawling all over the floor and across Jane's shoes. She tried not to look at them.

"I can stop you," Jane said.

"You can?"

Why isn't he scared? she thought. *He can't see it—remember, the*

Raven King doesn't even know what the Name of the World is. Jane's stomach spun in circles, her hands shook, and her legs felt weak.

"My grandmother beat you…"

"Yet, here I am," he said.

"You have to stop."

The Raven King was right in front of her. Jane smelled rotten fruit, and she tasted glue. There was cold terror in her belly. Her legs and arms and heart—every part of her wanted to run. She heard her pulse in both ears. She was breathing too fast.

"You are about to die, Jane," the Raven King said. "Just like your grandmother."

Jane raised the Name of the World—and he knocked it away. The mirror hit the wall and shattered into a thousand pieces.

CHAPTER 59

Jane and the Raven King

*N*o.

Jane stared at the slivers of broken glass all over the cavern floor. The tension in her stomach jumped to her chest, and she felt tears behind her eyes. She drew the black knife—but what was the point? *I've gone through so much,* she thought. *I came all this way for nothing. The Name of the World is ruined. I can't fight him now. I can't do anything.*

She looked at the rocks that had buried Finn and at Manali, who was still paralyzed on the floor. Jane felt dizzy. *I won't cry,* she told herself. The knife trembled in her hand. But this was really happening: She had lost. It was over.

"It's all right," the Raven King said. "You tried your best, but you are unarmed and helpless." When he touched Jane's shoulder, she started to cry. She couldn't move; she couldn't speak. Behind her, the sansi were creeping closer.

A hole opened in the ceiling of the cavern. The sky was blue with puffy white clouds. *That's topside Earth,* Jane thought. *That's the real world. The Raven King is about to go up there and turn everyone into his sansi slaves. He'll burn the cities the way he burned the Purple Marsh, and soon, everything will be brown and dead.*

"Now that it's over," the Raven King said, "will you help me?"

Jane stumbled backward. "What?"

"You don't have to die here, Jane. The world will be clean and ordered again. There are still children hiding from me—the ones who didn't hear my electric songs. But you and I know that they can't win. They belong to me. If you help me find them, I will give you anything you want. You must be hungry…" Behind the Raven King, there was suddenly a table full of food. Jane saw a Thanksgiving turkey, waffles, tacos, and chicken vindaloo. "And you like to read, don't you?" Full bookshelves—as tall as houses—appeared around the table. "Anything." Televisions and beanbag chairs and computers grew out of the cave floor.

"You can have anything in the world," the Raven King said. "Do you remember all those children at school who made fun of you? Do you remember the teachers who didn't like you? You can be the most popular person in school, Jane. You can be a queen. They'll worship you like a god. You can get back at them all if you want to."

Jane's mouth was dry as she continued to back away. Flies buzzed in her ears. Even though she could smell the wonderful food on the table, Jane could still taste something rotten on the back of her tongue, as if there were garbage buried under the floor.

"And I will give you one more thing if you help me, Jane," the Raven King said. "You can have your family back. I will spare your parents and your brother and even your grandmother. I'm offering you a good life. The Name of the World is gone. The mirror is destroyed. You have nothing. You can't win—but you don't have to lose. Will you help me?"

One hand tight on the black knife, Jane wiped sweat from her eyes. *He's right,* she thought. *I can't win now, but I can save my family. It's the smart thing to do, isn't it? Then why won't my arms stop shaking, and why won't my heartbeat slow down? I have to do what he wants to save Michael, Mom, and Dad—and Grandma Diana.* She opened her mouth to say yes.

"This is what you wanted, isn't it, Jane?" the Raven King said. "You want everything to go back to normal—but this will be even better than that."

Jane stared at the shattered fragments of the mirror. *The Name of the World is broken,* she thought. *I have to help my family.* Jane saw herself reflected in the glass shards, bloodied and dirt-streaked, the knife in one hand. The blade was bright in the reflection, as if the Sharp Map were white-hot. Strange, but she didn't have time to think. *Who would that make me if I help the Raven King? No. I still have the black knife. I have to fight him,* Jane told herself, *even though I'm going to lose—because otherwise, what good is it to be alive? Everything in the world may be chaos, but there's still right and wrong.*

Jane raised her knife and said, "No."

The cavern was empty again; the food, the bookshelves, the televisions—all of it was gone. The ceiling hole closed.

"I'm sorry, Jane," the Raven King said. "It's over."

He opened his hand, and a black beam lanced at Jane—she

turned and tripped over Thomas, and Grandma Diana's armor stopped the black light.

The Raven King was standing over her, his voice calm, "You are unarmed. And you are a fool." He leaned down slowly, his dark fingers reaching closer. "It will be over soon, child."

Jane tried to crawl backward, but when his hand touched her cheek, ice jolted in her heart and caught her breath. The world flashed black in a frozen rush that flooded Jane's chest, stomach, arms, and legs, up to her throat. She tried to scream, tasted blood, and drove the knife into the Raven King's chest. As he recoiled, air surged back into Jane's lungs, washing away the cold. The Raven King jerked, as if he'd been struck by lightning, and when she pulled out the blade, he screamed—it wasn't a human noise; it was the screech of a bird being crushed by a car. She stabbed him again. The Raven King exploded into a cloud of black birds that cawed and flapped in a whirlwind, thundering out of the cave.

The Raven King saw the mirror, Jane realized. That meant the mirror couldn't be the Name of the World. But the Raven King *didn't* see the black knife. Then what was the mirror? The broken pieces of the mirror should have reflected the ceiling or the walls; instead, they had reflected the black knife. She dropped the knife and slumped to her knees. Her hands were streaked with black blood. She smelled a zoo.

Someone said, "Our savior. Clear-Eyed Jane..."

The cave was packed with animals: horses, deer, rhinos, and bears all crowding her. The sansi had been transformed back. A pair of elephants cleared the rocks off of Finn. He rubbed his bruised head and said, "So what did I miss?"

"Jane?" a familiar voice said. The animals parted for Gaius and Grandma Diana. They were both smiling. "My Clear-Eyed Jane," Grandma Diana said. "Dear, you have saved us all."

CHAPTER 60

The World Restored

At the bottom of the Steel Mountain, all the trees had turned back into bobbins. There were beautiful female bobbins with golden fur and silver eyes, and young warrior bobbins in heavy armor and helmets. There were child bobbins that looked like serious, overdressed kittens. Gaius cast a spell that took them all back to the bobbin ruins—but they weren't ruins anymore. The overgrown stones had been transformed into proud, ivy-covered buildings that reminded Jane of an expensive college campus. The streets were shiny glass, and the grass was green and full of chattering animals. They were all waiting their turn to step inside the elevator and return to topside Earth so they could resume chasing and eating each other.

Gaius and Grandma Diana let Thomas go back too.

"The Raven King used this boy," Grandma Diana said, "the same way he tried to use you, Jane. It's not really his fault. But I knew all along that you wouldn't give in. Not my Jane. Did you get the envelope I sent with Miles?"

"I got it," Jane said.

"And you found the Name of the World with the Sharp Map on it, right where I left it all those years ago." Grandma Diana smiled at Gaius. They were standing at the elevator, watching the bobbins and animals rebuild part of the city.

"But all this time, I thought that mirror was the Name of the World," Jane said.

"The Diamond Mirror wasn't a weapon, Jane," Grandma Diana said. "Mirrors show us the world more clearly. The Raven King hid the Diamond Mirror in his cave because it can reveal the Name of the World to the right person. You saw the Name of the World in the mirror, didn't you?"

"Yes," Jane said. "The mirror reminded me that I could still fight back."

"You are welcome to stay here, you know," Gaius told Jane. "You don't have to go back."

Behind him, Finn called, "Now why would she want to do that?" Manali was riding on his back. "Down here, there are nothing but talking dragons and puffed-up cats. I mean, just look at all those cats! I think I liked them better as trees."

Manali said, "Finn!" She hopped down and gave Jane a hug.

"Thank you," Jane said.

"Hey, I didn't do much," Manali said. "I knew you'd save everybody. We all did—except Gaius and his tests."

Gaius cleared his throat. "Those three tests have a time-honored tradition—"

"—of picking the wrong kid and getting us all into trouble," Grandma Diana said.

They all laughed.

"Diana Starlight and Clear-Eyed Jane, you are welcome back any time," Gaius said. "And you too, Manali."

"Except you don't get a cool name, Manali," Finn muttered.

"I'm going to miss you, Jane," Manali said. "But you have my phone number, yeah?"

"Yes, I'll call you—I promise," Jane said. "And thank you for everything, Gaius. Finn…"

Finn farted a fireball. "I'm sorry," he said. "Were you saying something?" Finn hugged Jane with one massive paw. "No more good-byes—dragon tears are lethal."

Grandma Diana squeezed Jane's hand. "It's time to go."

As they went to the elevator, Jane asked, "Will Michael and Mom and Dad—will they all be okay?"

"Yes, dear. Everything is fixed because of you. The Raven King is gone." She brushed Jane's hair out of her eyes. "The real world is waiting. Don't be scared. It's going to be all right, I promise."

And it was.

Acknowledgments

I have to begin by thanking my wife, Ceceley, for her faith in me. It's no exaggeration to say that she made this possible. Thanks also to William and Ellie, for keeping me honest.

Huge thanks are due to my agent, Peter Rubie, for his commitment through all of these years and to my wonderful editor at Sourcebooks, Rebecca Frazer.

I am grateful to everyone who has helped and humored me since I began this project—you all know who you are.

About the Author

While still in high school, Stephen Chambers sold two novels, *Hope's End* and *Hope's War*. He has recently collaborated with bestselling author Adam Blade on *The Chronicles of Avantia*. Stephen is currently a doctoral candidate in the history department at Brown University.